Disarming Elena

A True North Ranch Story

**MOUNTAINS &
MAGNOLIAS**
PUBLISHING

Disarming Elena

A True North Ranch Story

TESSA LEIGH

Printed in the United States of America.

For information address:
Tessa Leigh Books
923 Oldham Drive, PO Box 384
Nolensville, TN 37135

Published by Mountains & Magnolias Publishing

Edited by Tri-Star Business Dynamics

ISBN: 979-8-9991894-1-7

First Edition June 2025

DEDICATION

To Liza,

For the young woman whose curiosity, joy, and love of story lit the way:
Your eagerness to read what I wrote, your questions, your laughter, your joy…
You sparked an ember in me I didn't know was waiting.
This one's for you.

Love,

Tessa

Table of Contents

Prologue

ELENA

The scent of kettle corn, dust, and hay hits me as soon as we step onto the rodeo grounds. I squint toward the grandstands where rows of families have gathered. There are kids with painted faces, teens clustered under the shade of the snack tent, old-timers already settling into their usual spots like time hasn't passed at all.

Jack walks a step behind me, close but not quite touching. We've grown used to each other's rhythm, but we're not fully in step yet.

A month ago, I wouldn't have imagined that I would be standing beside Jack Harrison at the Harmony County Rodeo, wearing jeans that fit and a tucked-in flannel I borrowed from Lisa. She'd thrust it at me with a grin and the words, "Local color matters," like it was gospel. And it is, out here. There's something about blending in that feels less like losing yourself and more like belonging. Like you've earned a place at the table just by showing up and being real.

Lisa says it's about respect. "You don't walk into someone else's story wearing city edges," she told me once. I'm starting to understand what she meant. The dust on your boots, the right shade of denim, knowing when to nod instead of speaking. It's not a costume. It's connection.

Lisa's somewhere near the livestock pens, doing exactly what she always does; making sure no one goes unseen. She's probably rallying the 4H kids, telling them their goats deserve equal camera time as the barrel racers. That's Lisa: cheerleader, firebrand, and walking press release.

She's lived here most of her adult life and seems to know everyone's grandmother, birth order, and livestock rotation. But it's not just about knowing people, it's about *lifting* them. She's made it her mission to shine light on the overlooked corners of this county, whether it's a fourth-grade art show or a junior high stock auction. She says stories matter, especially the ones that don't make headlines. And the more time I spend around her, the more I believe she's right.

Maybe that's why I've found myself leaning into the quieter routines lately, the trivial things that wouldn't make the news but still matter. The past month hasn't been quiet, not by a long shot. The sheriff's department is still tracking leads on the men who came after us.

Jack spends most mornings reviewing maps and grainy satellite photos like a man who knows the next move is coming, just not when. I spend mine in the chicken coop. Or what will be a chicken coop once Tom helps me finish the fencing. It's my way of building something steady, one plank at a time. I am working on creating a life that can't be stolen or shaken loose by fear.

Jack hasn't said no to the chickens, which, in his language, is practically a declaration of support.

He clears his throat beside me. "You sure you want to do this?"

I glance at the arena where the flag girls are warming up their horses, dust swirling around the hooves like smoke. "Attend the rodeo?"

"Be seen. Together."

I turn to look at him, sunlight catching in the few budding grays at the temples of his dark hair. "We already fought off a small militia together. I think we can survive a few curious glances."

He huffs a laugh, then tips his cowboy hat lower over his eyes. "Rodeo crowd might be tougher."

I nudge his arm with mine. "We've handled worse." I smile slyly at him, catching his eyes for a moment.

He doesn't move away. "Yeah," he says quietly. "But this… this feels bigger somehow."

The weight in his voice isn't fear, it's hope. Cautious, hard-earned, but real. I reach for his hand. "Then let's be seen."

He huffs a laugh, slipping his hand into mine, intertwining our fingers.

Lisa waves us over to the bleachers she staked out earlier. Tom's already there, a foam cup of lemonade balanced on his knee, boots dusty and his usual grin in place.

"Took you two long enough," he says, nodding to the two open seats beside him. "Was beginning to think the chickens came between you."

Jack lifts a brow at me. "Told you it was a bad idea to share my coffee with them."

"You're the one who started naming them," I fire back as I sit.

Tom chuckles, then leans toward me. "He named one Nugget," I laugh as I say it.

"Because she pecked through the feed sack like a drill sergeant," Jack mutters. "She's got spirit."

Lisa sits down with a bag of popcorn, giving me a sidelong smile. "You two planning on opening a bed and breakfast for barn animals, or are we going to get updates on the real stuff?"

The real stuff.

I glance around, scanning the crowd. No sign of danger. No shadows lurking behind the grandstands or out by the trailers. Still, I keep my phone in my pocket, set to silent but buzzing every few hours with an encrypted message from Sam who is now our reluctant informant. He hasn't revealed much yet, just hints. Symbols. Warnings. But it's enough to keep me watchful.

Jack must sense the shift in my body because his hand brushes mine. It's nothing overt, just the edge of his knuckle grazing mine like an anchor.

There's something kind in the way Jack makes space for me. And something steady in the way I find myself stepping into it. We've both agreed: whatever's growing between us needs to be real. Built slow. Honest.

We've barely held hands. There's too much to work through, too many tangled threads still hanging between the past and what might be next. But we both seem content to take it slow. To let the silence fill in where words aren't ready. Whatever this is becoming, it doesn't need to be hurried.

I'm sleeping in my old room, Declan's room, which feels both normal and not. The walls are familiar, the rhythm of the ranch settling into something that feels like home again. And yet, there's a shift I can't ignore. A quiet awareness, like a small ember lit deep in my chest, one that stirs every time Jack walks into a room or stands a little too close. He doesn't push. Neither do I.

Sometimes, late at night, I hear his boots on the porch, pacing. Other times, he leaves a mug of tea outside my door. We're not rushing anything. After what we both came through, trust is the most valuable thing we've got.

A cheer erupts as the rodeo announcer calls the start of the first event: junior roping. The kids are all elbows and nerves, their horses twitchy under the bright banners.

"Feels almost normal," Jack murmurs beside me, like he's afraid to name it too soon.

I smile, watching a girl no older than ten wrangle a calf like it's the most important thing she'll ever do. "It feels like hope."

He nods.

The sun is hot, the dust clings to everything, and still, I feel steady. Like, just maybe, we've earned this quiet moment.

But the fire isn't over. Not yet. And whatever comes next, we won't face it alone.

Chapter 1

Something in Between

ELENA

Jack is already in the coop, sleeves pushed to his elbows, brushing a handful of shavings from the nesting box floor.

"You always this productive before sunrise?" I ask as I approach, the bucket thumping lightly against my leg.

He glances up with a smirk. "Only when the company's good."

"Well, the hens seem to like you," I tease, nudging the gate shut behind me. "Even if you forgot to close the door again."

He laughs under his breath, a quiet, easy sound. "Maybe I was hoping you'd show up and scold me. Routine builds trust."

I arch a brow, but my grin gives me away. "Is that what this is? Chicken psychology?"

"Don't mock the method."

I shake my head as we both look out across the pasture. The fog is already lifting, the horizon warming. "So," I say after a beat, "you think we'll make it to the feed store and back before noon, or should we pencil in another flat tire?"

He groans. "One time. One flat. And I changed it faster than you could Google how."

"Still beat you at trivia while you were doing it."

"Yeah, yeah. I remember." and a smear of sawdust along his forearm from where he tightened the new latch. He doesn't look up right away, but I catch the way his shoulder shifts when he hears my boots crunch the gravel.

"You left the gate open," I say, nudging it shut with my foot. "You trying to teach them to fly?"

He straightens, squinting toward me through the early light. "They wouldn't get far. Nugget's too round to clear a breeze."

I grin as I pour the grain into the trough. The chickens descend like a tiny mob; clucking, pecking, squabbling over corn as if world peace depends on it. Jack leans against the doorframe of the coop, arms crossed, watching them with something close to amusement.

"They're the only things in my life that don't lie or carry weapons," I say lightly. The joke slips out on habit, but it hangs there longer than I expect. I try to swallow the aftertaste it leaves.

Jack's expression doesn't shift much, but I catch the flicker of something in his eyes. He doesn't push, just stoops to check the water dish instead.

I kneel in the dirt, brushing feed dust off my palms, and taking in the ranch around us. "Sometimes I wonder if this is real," I say. "Or just the breath we get before the next blow lands."

He straightens and dusts his hands on his jeans. "You've earned this pause."

"Have I?"

He doesn't answer right away. His gaze lingers on the chickens a little too long, like maybe he's seeing something else entirely. Memories he hasn't shared, regrets he doesn't have the words for. When he finally looks at me, there's a heaviness behind his eyes that makes my chest ache. Maybe silence is the only honesty either of us can manage right now.

"You okay?" I ask, though I already know the answer.

His gaze flicks down, and that's when I realize that he's not looking at me. He's looking at the T-shirt I borrowed from the laundry pile this morning. His old unit shirt. The faded insignia still visible across the front.

Something shifts in him. Not anger. Not surprise. Just... softness, threaded with something like sorrow.

"It's comfortable," I say quickly, fingers brushing the hem like it might explain everything. "Didn't think you'd mind."

3

"I don't," he says, voice low. The sound of his voice is like the words have to pass through something heavier before they reach me. "I just haven't seen that patch in a while."

I watch him. He's somewhere else now. Another time. Another version of himself. One that he has tried to leave behind, but the ghosts won't stay buried.

"You miss it?"

Jack takes a long breath. "Parts of it. People. Purpose. But the rest..." He trails off, then shakes his head. "Not enough to go back." He pauses, eyes scanning the trees like he's remembering something just out of reach. "Declan and I did walk away, eventually. We bought this land outside of Colorado Springs, eighty acres adjacent to the twenty my dad left me. Back then, most of it was wild. We started fencing the pastures ourselves, converting the old barn, talking about longhorns and mustangs like it was a second language. We were building something real. Simple. Honest." He swallows hard. "Declan took a few more missions, even after we broke ground. Then he didn't come back."

I nod, but my chest tightens. We're standing on that land now. It is what was supposed to be the beginning of something steady, something earned, something that would help other veterans.

I remember the early sketches, the arguments between them over where the ranch house should go, the way Declan would run his hands over the rough timber like he could see the finished dream. I wasn't always in it the way they were, but I was still part of the dream. And now it's just Jack, carrying the weight of what they started and never got to finish. What parts of him are still building? What parts stopped the day Declan died?

Standing on this very porch after the ambush and fallout last month, we said we'd face whatever Declan left behind. And maybe we believed it. Just enough to start laying foundations again.

4

Chickens, fences, quiet mornings. But the weight of what Declan knew, what he left behind, still hangs in the air like the smell of smoke after a fire.

Some mornings, I think we're still standing in that smoke.

Jack doesn't say it, but I see the tension in his shoulders when the wind shifts or when headlights flash too long on the county road. I feel it in myself too, in the way I check locks twice, the way my hand hovers just a second too long over the drawer where we keep the loaded Glock.

Whatever this place becomes, it's rooted in what we lost. Built on memories, grief, and the kind of love that doesn't vanish just because someone is gone. And maybe that's what makes it hard to name. It could be sacred or haunted, or something in between.

Chapter 2

Circled in Red

JACK

The map unfolds between us on the kitchen table, the creases still stiff from where it had been hidden away; folded tight and buried in the false bottom of Declan's gear case. The paper smells like dust and old leather, like time that should've stayed locked away.

I don't say anything at first. I just flatten it out with both hands, letting her see it. Letting her draw her own conclusions before I offer any.

Elena crosses the room slowly, her coffee forgotten in one hand. She doesn't sit. Just stares.

"Declan's?" she asks.

I nod. "Yes, from a safe house in Kentucky. Found it rolled into a field journal. I brought it back shortly after he died, but I hadn't opened it until just recently. After the ambush."

She leans in, her eyes sweeping over the notations, examining the coordinates, circles, arrows, initials. Her brows pull together. Then she spots it.

A name.

My name.

The silence changes. It's no longer just heavy. Now it's personal. Confused. Wary. She doesn't ask why Declan had been tracking me. Doesn't accuse. Just stands there in the quiet, jaw clenched.

Before I can say anything, a truck rumbles up the gravel drive. Through the window, I spot Tom easing out, oversized Carhartt jacket zipped to his chin, one hand holding a thermos, the other a white bakery box.

Broad-shouldered and steady as ever, he's the kind of man who never raises his voice and always shows up when it counts; ranch hand, former Army, part of the backbone around here. He'd been my dad's friend before mine, but somewhere along the way, he became family.

My dad had moved from eastern Colorado to western Colorado shortly after Declan and I graduated from high school. Tom had been the first friend he made here, and when my dad passed, Tom stepped in like an uncle. Making sure Declan and I had an anchor and guide when we decided we wanted to purchase land in this same area and build a refuge. I inherited Dad's twenty acres, then bought the other eighty adjacent to it.

"Tom," I say, standing. "He's early."

I slide the map back into the drawer as the front door swings open without a knock.

"Mornin'," Tom calls. "Hope I'm not crashing anything. I come bearing peace offerings."

Elena steps forward from the kitchen's far corner, already reaching for a plate. "If those are cinnamon rolls, you can crash anytime."

Tom grins and sets the box down. "Fresh from the diner. Thought you two could use something sweet this morning."

He opens the lid to reveal half a dozen oversized rolls dripping with glaze. The smell of warm sugar and spice wrapping around us instantly, like a blanket. Elena's whole face softens. She takes one without hesitation and tears into it like she hasn't eaten all week.

"These are unreal," she says around a bite. Eating it with what can only be described as bliss.

Tom chuckles. "I overestimated my willpower. Figured it was safer to share than to end up in a sugar coma alone."

We all sit. I claim the head of the table, Elena on my right, Tom across from her. The box sits between us, already down two rolls.

For a minute, there's only chewing and the quiet creak of chairs. Then Tom sips from his thermos and says, "First time I met Declan, I didn't know what to make of him."

That gets my attention.

Tom continues, "He was polished, you know? Knew how to carry a conversation, how to make people comfortable. At first, I thought maybe he was trying a little too hard."

He glances toward Elena and softens his tone. "But over time, I saw something shift in him. Like he was tired of pretending. Like he wanted to be real. Especially around you two."

Elena looks down at her roll, suddenly very still.

Tom shifts in his seat. "I don't know what happened at the end. But for a while there? I think he was trying to do better. Be better."

My jaw tightens, but I nod. It's the most generous read of Declan I've heard in a long time. Maybe the most accurate, too.

Tom looks at me again. "You, on the other hand, never had much patience for pretending."

I huff a dry breath. "Didn't seem useful."

"No," Tom agrees. "But it made you the one holding things together, even when you were coming apart."

We fall quiet again.

After a few minutes, Tom stands and brushes cinnamon from his jacket. "I'll let you two get back to your morning. Just wanted to check in."

He pauses at the door. "If Elena ever needs a break, my mom would love to have her over. She makes a mean pot of tea and never runs out of things to talk about."

Elena smiles faintly. "Thank you. I might take you up on that."

Tom tips his head. "You'd be welcome."

He steps out, the door clicking shut behind him.

I stay at the table a little longer, eyes drifting to the drawer where the map is tucked away. The cinnamon roll in front of me has gone cold, untouched.

Declan left more than just secrets. He left questions. Shadows. And if that map means what I think it does…

He might've also left a trail.

And we're standing at the edge of it.

Chapter 3

Hints of Betrayal

ELENA

The light filters through the porch slats in thin, golden lines that stretch across the floorboards, like the day is trying to reach in and pull me forward. The swing creaks beneath me, slow and steady, as I sit cross-legged with a warm mug in my hands. The front porch faces west, toward the low-slung ridge of the Rockies. In the distance, the sun edges toward the horizon, casting long shadows across the pasture where the chickens scratch under the fence line and the cattle graze just beyond. It's a scene that feels borrowed from someone else's life. It's peaceful, still, almost too fragile to be real.

But of course, I'm thinking about the map we had out on the kitchen table.

Not just about the red mark by Jack's name, or the ghost symbol beside it, but about something else. Something older. Something I've carried a long time.

"You ever wonder," I say, not looking at him, "how many near-misses we've had?"

Jack is sitting on the steps below, elbows on his knees, turning a bolt in his hand like he's trying to remember what it's for. "All the time."

"I mean before all this. Before you and I even knew each other."

He glances up. "You thinking of something specific?"

I nod, staring past the fence, toward where the wind moves the tall grass in waves. "There was a mission. Not mine, at least not officially. I was trying to help someone I shouldn't have trusted. Smuggling data through a contact in Dubrovnik. Thought it was just relocation documents, nothing flagged."

Jack's whole-body stills. Quiet, measured. Listening like a man who already knows what comes next.

"I walked into the wrong safehouse. Two men, both armed and edgy, were already there. One grabbed my arm before I could speak. The other stepped out of the shadows like he'd been there all along, and I swear, Jack... he didn't flinch. Didn't blink. Just said,

'She's not the one. Let her go.' And the guy obeyed, like something in the second man's voice rewrote the rules."

Jack doesn't respond. Not yet. His jaw tightens just enough to tell me I'm not imagining it. There's something there that he knows. Something that he is holding on to.

"I never saw him again. He disappeared before I could even ask his name." I look down at him. "That was you, wasn't it?"

Gazing out at the mountains, he exhales through his nose, slow and heavy. "Yes."

I study him, but the porch tilts slightly beneath me. Something fundamental just came unmoored.

"You were there." The words taste strange. I don't know if it's a question or an accusation. "Why didn't you tell me?" I am not angry, but I am unsettled.

"Because it wasn't supposed to be you." He sets the bolt down like it suddenly weighs too much. "You weren't flagged. Not then. You were supposed to be a civilian with a questionable file, and I was there to verify assets and shut down the threat."

"And I was the threat?"

"Almost." His voice cracks slightly. "Someone put your name on a shortlist, Elena. If I hadn't been there… it would've gone very differently."

The porch creaks as I shift forward in the swing, placing my feet on the porch floor. "You knew. All these years?" I press the mug against my chest, trying to still the sudden thrum under my ribs. He let me walk around all this time thinking that maybe I was foolish for

13

remembering the way that voice felt like safety. Like recognition. I didn't imagine it. And he let me. "And you never said anything?"

He looks up at me, regret clear in his brown eyes. "I didn't know how. And later, when everything with Declan happened... it didn't feel like something to drop between grief and survival."

I stare past him, to the edge of the north field where the old barn leans into the low angle of the sunset, its weathered boards glowing faintly in the amber light, and wildflowers push through the wire.

"I should've asked more questions."

"I should've given you answers."

We sit in silence, the kind that stretches between memory and now. The kind that can break or bind, depending on what you do next.

After a moment, I speak again, quieter this time. "Did you follow me after that?"

He shakes his head. "No. I wasn't allowed to. But I flagged your file. Quietly. Kept an eye out when I could. Then I lost you in the system."

"So you watched me from a distance?"

He doesn't deny it. "No. But I always remembered you... I knew it was you when we met again. I didn't expect to. But I remembered. You don't forget someone who walks out of a death trap."

"Everything clicked."

"Yeah," he takes a deep breath, "Then Declan…"

The silence settles like ash. I sip my coffee, but it's gone lukewarm. In this moment, I don't care. I tuck my feet beneath me, trying to figure out how to sit with a past I didn't know I had. I don't know what to do with this kind of truth, this kind of history rewritten in one conversation.

And then he says, "That job… that mission you walked into, it wasn't random. The files Declan had, the threads we're pulling now… I think it's all connected."

My blood goes cold.

"Connected how?"

"I don't know yet. But you were never just collateral, Elena. You were already in it. We just didn't know what 'it' was yet."

Before I can respond, Jack's phone buzzes, sharp and sudden in the quiet. He checks the screen, his body tensing in an instant.

"Who is it?" I ask.

I catch the change in his demeanor; shoulders drawn tighter, that faraway edge sharpening in his eyes. He looks at me, and for a second, I think he might lie.

But he doesn't. Not yet.

He rises to his feet slowly, the porch groaning under his weight. "Denton. One of my old contacts from the Kyiv operation. We haven't spoken in months. He handles special…" he turns to look at me as he walks away, "Situations."

15

He answers, a clipped greeting, and I watch his posture shift as he listens. Whatever he hears on the other end, it carves the calm right off his face.

When he hangs up, I'm already bracing. "Talk to me, Jack."

"He's talking," Jack says, tapping the phone against in his hand, nervously. "Rook. He served with Declan and I for years."

I frown. "I remember the name, but nothing about him."

Jack nods. "He's a wounded warrior in more ways than one. He's having a rare lucid moment and naming names now. And one of them might be connected to the network Declan flagged."

Something pulses in the space between us. Recognition. Dread.

"We're not chasing ghosts anymore," I say.

Jack meets my eyes. "No. We're walking straight into the fire."

And for the first time in days, I don't feel like I'm drowning in the unknown. I feel like we're finally choosing to face it.

Together.

Somewhere behind us, the kitchen clock ticks on. The sun continues its slow descent over the Rockies. And whatever comes next, it's already in motion.

Chapter 4

Broken

JACK

Officially designated as the Behavioral Evaluation Unit, the facility is hidden deep along a narrow canyon road just north of the Wyoming state line. Cloaked by scrub pine and forgotten utility lines, it doesn't draw attention, which is exactly the point. This place was built to contain mentally fractured military assets, especially those carrying classified intel too dangerous to bleed into civilian life.

We don't speak much on the drive. Sometimes the quiet between us brings a level of peace I don't get anywhere else.

The road winds tighter the farther we get from anything recognizable. There are no signs, no cell signal, just dirt switchbacks and the occasional deer flashing through the brush.

About a mile out, I slow the truck and glance sideways. "Elena. There's something you should know before we go in."

She turns to me, alert. "Alright."

"Rook. It's not his real name, obviously. I knew him when he was still in the field. He was in the military then black ops. He did insertion work, deep reconnaissance, and high-risk intercepts. He was good. Smart. Not the brute kind of asset. He spoke four languages, played classical violin, used to quote philosophy while wiring surveillance feeds."

She raises an eyebrow. "Doesn't sound like the guy we're walking into."

"He's not," I admit. "That version of him didn't survive what came next. About four years ago, he was burned during a covert in Mogilev. Someone sold his location, maybe a leak, maybe intentional, and his entire team got wiped. He was the only one pulled out. Spent six months off-grid after extraction. When they found him, he barely spoke."

Elena swallows hard. "PTSD?"

"Among other things," I say. "Whatever they did to him, it wasn't just physical, it was psychological. He's fractured. Jumpy. And he only responds to a few names. Mine happens to be one of them, and only sporadically."

She nods, grip tightening around the folder in her lap. The folder goes anywhere we do when there is a possibility of needing reference to it. I made a copy and buried it on the ranch where I can find it if needed, but for now, the one in Elena's hands is the only one anyone knows about.

"I remember you and Declan talking about him. For whatever reason, his name stuck with me. Even after all these years."

"He might not recognize me. Or he might recognize something we don't know he saw. Either way... just be ready. You're not walking into a cell. You're walking into what's left of a man who was once one of the best we had."

Inside, the air is stale. Metallic. Like too many secrets have been kept here too long.

I lead Elena through two layers of reinforced doors until we reach the room where they are keeping him. It's less of a room and more of a chamber. A flickering overhead light casts harsh shadows across the room. There's a chair with restraints still hanging loosely from it, a table, and the man they call Rook, seated like a caged animal, coiled and wary.

He's thinner than I remember. His frame gaunt, twitchy. Sweat darkens the collar of his shirt even though the room is cold. His eyes track every movement we make.

"Rook," I say, calm and measured.

He doesn't look up.

I pull the map from my jacket and lay it flat on the table.

That gets a reaction.

Rook's gaze snaps to the paper. His fingers tremble. "Where did you get that?"

19

"Declan's files," I answer. "You know what it is."

Silence. Then a whisper.

"Ledger... T-6... Voss."

The words land like smoke; faint, drifting, but impossible to ignore.

"Tell me what they mean."

His lips twitch, trying to conjure the words. Then he sees Elena.

Something in his expression fractures. His shoulders curl in. A flinch, sharp and involuntary, like he's seen a ghost. Perhaps something worse.

"Do you recognize her?" I ask, stepping between them.

Rook shakes his head too fast, too many times. "No... I didn't know. I didn't know she was involved." He starts rocking.

Elena freezes beside me. "Involved in what?"

But it's already too late. Rook folds inward, lips clamped shut, breath coming short and ragged.

Whatever he saw on that map, or in her, was enough to shut him down.

I exhale slowly, hand dragging through my hair.

Before I can say more, a metal door creaks open behind us. A man steps inside, mid-fifties, military cut, eyes that never stop moving.

"Denton," I say, straightening.

He nods. "He's done for today. His vitals are spiking, and the doc says if we push, we will lose him again. We never know how long."

"So, he's still yours?" Elena asks. "Not being transferred?"

"For now," Denton says. "But if command gets wind that he dropped the name Voss, they'll pull him somewhere deeper than this and bury the rest. You've got maybe a day. Maybe two if I lean hard."

I look down at the map, still spread across the table. "That's not enough." I fold the map and tuck it under my arm heading toward Denton standing at the door.

"It never is," Denton replies. He glances at Elena, and something flickers across his face. Perhaps its recognition, maybe something else.

Denton hesitates at first. "You were in Rijeka, weren't you?"

Elena stiffens. "Excuse me?"

"Rijeka. 2018. The orphanage fire that wasn't." Denton crosses his arms. "There were rumors. A female contact got burned in the intel fallout. You're not just a widow in the wrong place at the wrong time. You were in the field."

She doesn't answer, but her silence says enough.

Denton grunts. "Then you know what's at stake." He nods at us, before he turns to check on Rook and closes the door behind us.

Elena and I step into a narrow corridor lined with cold cinderblock and buzzing fluorescents.

"T-6," she says quietly. "That wasn't just a code name, was it?"

21

I shake my head. "No. It was the designation for deep-cover intel ops, layers above my clearance. Stuff so compartmentalized, most agents didn't even know it existed."

"And Declan knew."

I nod. "He had to. That map, those symbols, they weren't just intel markers. They were warnings. He was chasing something big. Bigger than I realized."

Her voice drops lower. "If Declan was chasing this… what the hell was he trying to stop?"

We don't say it out loud, but we're both thinking it: the sealed envelope Sam delivered, the random deed. The way Declan's life bled into mine before I even knew it.

None of this is coincidence.

And someone, perhaps Rook, or maybe Denton, knows more than they're saying.

We're running out of time.

Chapter 5

A Voice From the Past

JACK

I'd avoided the flash drive. Not because I couldn't crack it, but because I wasn't ready for what I might find. Declan's last breadcrumb. I'd pocketed it during the chaos at the ambush site; when the gunfire cleared and the smoke was still thick. I didn't turn it over to the sheriff, didn't mention it in the debrief. I told myself it was instinct. Truth was, I needed to know what Declan hadn't said, and this was the only way to hear it. It sat in the back of the drawer next to the spare batteries and broken pens, just close enough to remind me it was there, just far enough to ignore.

Until now.

Elena leans over the table beside me, her blonde hair pulled into a messy knot, one of my sweatshirts loose around her shoulders. The same one she stole last week when the wind cut across the prairie in those straight-line gusts that rattled the windows and slipped past every doorframe. The trees around the house dulled most of it, but not enough to stop the chill from finding her shoulders. I never asked for it back, maybe because a part of me liked the way it looked on her.

I ground myself quickly realizing that I have been looking too long. She's smart and getting smarter every day. Leaving her shell behind. Like a butterfly coming out of a cocoon.

The jump drive looks normal, except for the warping in the housing, like it was too close to a heat source once. The night of the ambush it was cold and rainy, so it must have been before that. I roll it between my fingers, inspecting it.

"You sure you want to open this?" she asks, fingers drumming lightly near the laptop's edge.

"No," I answer honestly. "But I think it was meant for him, and he never got the chance. Someone passed it off, or maybe it was taken after. Either way, it found us. And I don't believe in accidents like that."

Elena is quiet for a moment, then says, "Sam delivered that envelope, the night of the ambush He wouldn't tell me who gave it to him."

I glance at her. "You think it came from the same source?"

"I think it's all the same trail," she says. "Different pieces, same hands."

She nods once. I enter the final string of keys, and the screen flickers.

Two folders appear when the drives loads: **VOSS** and **THORNE_BLACK_LEDGER**.

Elena's breath catches. "Voss. That was one of the names Rook dropped."

I click the folder. Inside: a few short, corrupted audio files. The filenames are gibberish, but one plays cleanly. I hit it.

Declan's voice fills the room. Grainy, clipped.

Elena jerks slightly, like she's been slapped by the sound. Her breath catches, and for a second I think she might tell me to stop the playback. But she doesn't. She just closes her eyes.

I don't move until she opens them again. Here eyes are wet, but clear. Then I shift, close enough to wrap an arm gently around her shoulders, leaving just enough space for her to lean into my side if she wants. No words. Just quiet presence, steady and sure.

We both lost him. But hearing his voice again cuts in ways neither of us has figured out how to talk about yet, especially now.

"If this gets out… someone close goes down. I don't know who to trust. Not even…"

The rest distorts into static.

I don't realize I've gripped the edge of the table until Elena places a hand on mine. Grounding.

I close the file and open the second folder.

Scans. Logs. Redacted field reports with half-erased names. One symbol repeats across several pages; a diamond inside a broken ring.

Elena leans in. "I've seen that before."

I glance at her.

"Years ago. Dubrovnik. It was stamped on a file I wasn't supposed to see. I didn't know what it meant then."

Now we do. The symbol's right there, stamped across half a dozen intel logs. And it's the same shape she'd seen in that file all those years ago. Now it's tied to Declan's voice, to ghost ops, to Voss. To everything that's suddenly pointing back to us somehow; the names, the ops, the symbol. Rook recognized her, the map had my name on it, and now this drive is filled with pieces only we seem to fit. It's not just data. It's a trail, and it's circling us.

She scrolls through the files slowly, silently. I watch her expression shift with recognition, dread, then something colder.

"This ledger," she murmurs. "It's not just about funding. These are names. Shell identities. Ghost agents."

My throat tightens. "Declan died for this."

Elena nods, eyes still on the screen. "And someone out there still wants it buried."

I shut the laptop.

For a moment, all I can hear is the wind outside. The distant, low bawl of a restless cow. The kettle clicking as it cools on the stove.

"We're in it now," she says.

I reach for her hand again, not to pull her in, just to hold steady. "We always were."

Sam might have answers. He brought Elena that envelope, he must know something.

Chapter 6

Missing Pieces

ELENA

I don't sleep that night. Not really. Every time I close my eyes, I hear Declan's voice in that clipped recording, the way it cut off like a final breath. Like he was about to say something that could have changed everything.

By morning, the air carries that ominous stillness that settles when the mountains trap a system as it comes across the Front Range. The clouds stretch wide across the open sky, heavy and unmoving, the kind that gather like a held breath, warning more than threatening, but not for long. I find Jack already outside, tightening a hinge on the barn gate like muscle memory is the only thing keeping him steady.

He doesn't look up when I approach. "Did you get any sleep?"

"No. You?"

He shakes his head. "Hard to, with the wind and everything else."

I nod, hugging my arms tighter across my chest. "This place is quiet, but not silent." I take a deep breath and turn to look at him, "At least with both of us under the same roof, it's easier to breathe."

His eyes turn to mine. "Separate rooms. Shared walls. It's not much, but… it helps."

There's no heat behind the words, just a quiet truth. We're taking it slowly for all the right reasons. But there's comfort in the nearness. A sense of safety that comes from knowing the other is just a hallway away.

He shakes his head again, slower this time. Not just about sleep, but about everything. Like the weight of Declan's voice, the uncertainty, and the storm gathering outside is all pressing down at once, and he can't quite shrug it off.

I step beside him, my arms wrapped tight against the wind curling over the prairie. "That voice memo… it sounded like Declan was trying to warn someone."

Jack nods. "Or confess." He glances at me then, searching my face, like he's trying to read what I'm thinking but not sure if he has the right. He watches for a beat longer than usual, quietly gauging if this changes anything between us.

The silence stretches between us, thick with questions neither of us wants to speak yet.

"I keep thinking," I say quietly, "what if he meant you? What if you were the one he couldn't trust?"

Jack stills. For a beat, I wonder if I've crossed a line I can't step back from. But when he turns to me and takes a step forward, his eyes are steady. "Then I'd want to know why."

The honesty in that answer undoes something in me. Not because I think Declan was right, but because Jack isn't running from it. He's facing it like he always does.

Head-on.

He brushes a hand over the top rail of the fence, staring out at the pasture. "You know what haunts me?" he says quietly. "It's not what I did overseas. It's not even losing Declan. It's that there are pieces missing. There are things I should've seen but didn't. And now we're standing in the aftermath trying to build a picture from fragments."

Later that afternoon, Jack takes the truck into Colorado Springs to meet an old contact from his unit. He leaves the laptop hidden and a brief note on the counter: "Just sharing intel. Back before dark."

Jack doesn't come back.

By nightfall, panic blooms in my chest. I try his phone twice and get nothing. The third time, it rings and rings before dumping me to voicemail.

I pace the house for twenty minutes, then dig out the emergency burner phone and encrypted laptop Jack set up after the ambush. It's a private fallback system he never explained, only said to use if things ever felt wrong. Right now, things feel very wrong.

I boot up the machine and connect to the shadow network Jack used during his last ops. It's an old military-grade channel, buried beneath layers of misdirection and ghost protocols. I'm rusty, but the instincts kick in fast. I follow ping trails and scrubbed access logs, tracking location metadata across ghosted government nodes.

And I find him.

He's being held in a temporary black site facility that is off grid, but not untouchable. Internal threat assessment flagged him as a potential leak inside a compartmentalized unit.

Before I leave the ranch, I change into dark jeans and a fitted jacket. Something that is neutral and forgettable. I double-check the locks, bolt every door, and slide one of Jack's spare handguns into the holster under my jacket. A knife in my boot. Quiet. Deliberate.

I drive through the night; tension coiled in my chest. When I reach the checkpoint, I show them the old contact code Jack once made me memorize. It's the kind of code that doesn't just get attention; it gets escalation.

"Tell your supervisor Elena Dawson is here," I say. "And if that doesn't mean anything to you, tell him I said Denton's watching."

That gets movement.

The man behind the desk stiffens, then reaches for a line that rings direct to someone. No keypad, no buttons. It's just a red handset on a land line; the kind reserved for silent authority and classified orders.

31

Every instinct in me wants to pace the floor, but I hold myself in place. Projecting confidence, but not arrogance. I know that this facility is wired with eyes and ears, and I am not going to show a flinch of emotion other than what I want them to see.

After a few tense minutes, the controlled door buzzes open and Jack steps through, flanked by two agents. His hands are free, but his jaw is tight, shoulders squared like he's daring them to try something.

They stop a few feet from me. One of the agents gives a clipped nod. "He's been cleared for release." No apology. No explanation. The first one turns and goes back to the door, but the second one crosses his arms across his chest and watches us leave.

Jack doesn't speak until we are in the jeep and headed away from the facility.

"They flagged me based on Declan's map," he says, voice low as we drive. "Thought I knew too much."

"What did you give them?" I ask.

He glances at me, just once. "I said one name: Isaac Voss."

Two agents had questioned him. They had both been stone-faced, well-trained, and gave nothing away. But when he said that name, they glanced at each other. Just once. Tight. Sharp. Controlled. Then silence. They shut down the line of questioning and ended the session early.

That one look told him more than the entire interrogation ever could.

Back home hours later, Jack sits beside me at the kitchen table, fingers steepled under his chin.

"Someone inside doesn't want the truth about Declan, or this 'Black Ledger,' getting out."

I look at the flash drive. Then at him.

"So we stop reacting," I say.

He nods. "We start hunting. First breadcrumb, starting with M. Thorne."

I lean back, the storm still simmering outside but something colder settling in my chest now: resolve.

We're done waiting.

Now we dig.

Chapter 7

Ghosts of the Past

JACK

The wind at the ranch has quieted, but everything else hums with unease. We've slept little, eaten less. The flash drive sits in front of us like it's waiting to be opened again; like it knows we're not done yet.

I pull up the folder labeled **THORNE_BLACK_LEDGER** and begin cross-referencing the fragments of documents. Names, call signs, scattered field notes. The formatting is inconsistent. Some are typed, some scanned in shaky handwriting.

"Thorne," I murmur. "Is it a person, alias, or designation?"

Elena leans over my shoulder, scanning the fragments with me. "If it's an alias, it's well used. This one here links it to a funding transfer in Kosovo. And this..." she taps another file, "this mentions an op that lists Declan under secondary clearance."

I frown. "He never mentioned it. Not by name. But I remember once that he said there was someone who oversaw the clean-up. A ghost contact. Someone even command tiptoed around."

"Thorne," she echoes quietly.

I open another file. Corrupted, mostly unreadable. But tucked near the bottom is a reference to T-6.

Elena goes quiet for a beat, her brows pulling in as something clicks behind her eyes. "Wait," she says. "Back when I moved, I packed one of Declan's old range bags. I remember finding a jump drive inside, but I didn't think it was important, but I threw it in the safe at my apartment thinking one day I would look at it."

I straighten. "Is it still there?"

She nods slowly. "Yeah. I haven't touched the safe since."

"Then we go now."

Getting in the truck, there is a heaviness about the air and it's not a fall storm moving in. To lighten the weight in the cab, I nod toward the southern field we pass near the edge of the ranch. "See that dead cottonwood near the creek? High ground past that used to be the best place for watching trail movement. Declan called it 'the perch.' We should think about running a secondary fence line that way. We could get better visibility, and easier to keep the creek from becoming a weak point in the perimeter."

Elena follows my gaze and nods. "Makes sense. Might be good for the new calf too. That is if Nugget ever stops bullying him."

That earns a laugh from me. "She's got more attitude than the rest of the chickens combined. I caught her chasing the wheelbarrow yesterday."

"She's establishing dominance," Elena says with a smile. "Future queen of the barnyard."

The drive to Colorado Springs is just under thirty minutes, the silence broken by the hum of tires and the occasional gust of wind across the open highway.

About halfway there, Elena turns slightly in her seat, looking out the window, watching the western horizon. A storm that rolled through overnight left a silver crown of snow on Pikes Peak. The sky is clear now, a soft blaze of gold and lavender brushing the mountains.

"It's weird," she says. "How quiet things feel, even when everything's wrong."

I glance at her, keeping one hand on the wheel, the other on the center console. "Sometimes quiet is just the breath before the noise."

She smiles faintly, then lets out a soft laugh. "That sounds like something Declan would've said."

I nod. "It was. But it fits you better now."

That earns a glance. Not playful, not surprised, just searching. "You think I'm changing?"

"I think you're stepping into who you always were."

She doesn't answer right away, and I don't push. But the way her hand rests between us on the console, close, unspoken, I don't move mine either. Not yet.

By the time we reach her apartment, the mood has shifted. It is still serious, but not brittle.

The building is quiet, tucked between a row of aging units with weathered siding and narrow balconies. Elena's apartment faces east, toward the wide-open plains, toward the direction of the ranch. She once told me she chose it for that reason, knowing full well she couldn't see the ranch from here, but needing to feel oriented toward something that had once felt like home. Like the True North Ranch was her beacon.

Inside, the space is clean but sparse. A threadbare couch sits angled toward the window, its fabric worn and sun faded. There's a bookshelf half-filled with titles she probably meant to read and never quite got around to. A pair of framed photos lean against the wall instead of hanging on it. One of them is Declan in his dress uniform. The second picture of her and a dog I don't recognize.

She moves with a quiet purpose, retrieving the drive and locking the safe again. But before we leave, she pauses. Her eyes sweep the small apartment slowly, like she's seeing it through new eyes.

"I'll grab a few things," she says.

She disappears into the back, returning a few minutes later with a duffel bag. A few folded shirts. A jacket. An extra pair of riding boots. She doesn't say she's coming back to permanently stay at the ranch, but it's in the way she moves, the way she zips the bag closed like she's sealing off a chapter.

She catches me watching and shrugs. "I was surviving here. Not really living."

37

And I know what she means. She'd been making it work, but just barely. For a long time, she had been stuck in grief, circling through days that didn't give her much to hold onto.

Whatever this is between us, it's not just about survival anymore.

We're silent on the way back, both of us weary and watching the road with the kind of focus that isn't just about driving. It's apprehension, about what we'll find, what we've already uncovered, and what comes next. The humor from earlier has faded, but something steady remains. We're not alone in this. Not anymore.

Back at the ranch house, we settle in. The wind has grown quiet again, and the flash drive she retrieved sits between us on the table like it's been waiting. Before we get started, Elena brings us both fresh coffees.

We plug it in.

Before the scan fully loads, Elena points to the file name at the top corner of the preview window. "That string of initials, M.J., I've seen those before."

I glance at her. "Where?"

"Sunday newspaper," she says dryly, and I almost laugh, but her eyes are serious. "No, I saw them on a manifest Declan left on the dining table when he got back from El Paso. I didn't think much of it at the time. Just initials. But now... I think they were tied to a handler. Maybe even Thorne."

"M.J." I repeat it under my breath. "We need to find out who that is."

Inside is one file. A scan that has faded, but unmistakably real. Handwritten. Pages from something that feels older than the agency itself.

"The Black Ledger," Elena says under her breath.

She scrolls carefully. The handwriting changes between entries. They're coded, paranoid, and maybe desperate. Near the bottom of one page, we find it:

T-6 = field asset. Handler: M. Thorne. Do not expose.

Elena goes still beside me. "Do not expose?"

We stare at the line together, the weight of it landing like a trap closing.

She meets my gaze. "What kind of operation needs a warning like that?"

I don't answer. Not yet. But a thought is forming.

"Elena," I say slowly, "Do you remember that envelope Sam gave you?"

Her eyes narrow slightly. "The one after Declan died?"

"Yeah. Now we know the flash drive came from someone with access. But if that envelope also came from inside..."

She leans back slightly. "Then Sam's contact was part of this too. Or being used by someone who was."

That same symbol, a diamond inside a broken ring, appears again in the margin of the scan. Marked in faded red ink like a silent watermark.

She points to it. "Same mark as before."

"It's following us," I murmur.

"No," she says. "It's watching us."

Chapter 8

They're Watching

ELENA

The next morning, we split up. Jack disappears into the shed with one of Declan's old burner phones, tracing the encrypted call logs left behind on the flash drive. I stay inside, poring over the scanned pages from the Black Ledger, trying to find anything that connects the T-6 entry to something human. Something nameable.

He returns just after noon, windblown and tight jawed, a folded piece of notepaper in hand. "Got something. One of the comm strings connects to a border town safehouse Declan flagged three years ago."

"M. Thorne?" I ask.

Jack nods. "Last known contact. If anyone can make sense of what Declan was chasing, it's him."

We head out again, this time south toward the Texas and New Mexico border near El Paso. The drive is long, and somewhere past Las Cruces, the conversation drifts into the kind of quiet that feels earned.

Along a stretch of dessert, Jack gestures to the stretch of highway ahead. "This road used to be a trafficking route," he says. "Years ago. Before the border tech improved. Smugglers used it because it was so remote. Easy to stash cargo and vanish into the hills."

I glance out the window. It doesn't look like much now, just asphalt cracked by time and heat, but the idea of what used to run beneath our tires makes my skin tighten.

"Still feels like it holds ghosts," I murmur.

Jack nods once, eyes on the road. "Some places don't forget."

The closer we get to the border, the more the mountains shift and become less jagged, more sprawling. Ridges give way to mesas, and the peaks turn into long, dusty hills. The land doesn't flatten so much as stretch out into something older, quieter.

The safehouse sits on the edge of a forgotten highway outside of El Paso. It's just a one-story adobe shell with sun-bleached paint and boarded windows. No mailbox. No sign. The kind of place people drive past without remembering.

Inside, the air smells like dust and rust. Everything that could be shredded, burned, or smashed has been. Fragments of maps. Bits of burned plastic. A half-melted phone. And then, on the floor near a collapsed shelf, Jack finds it; a small medallion, bronze and tarnished, with a symbol etched into the back.

T-6.

He holds it out to me, and I swallow hard.

Jack and I stare at it, then each other for a moment. Shock turns to realization. "It's real," I whisper.

In the back room, I check the bathroom and next to the mirror something catches my eyes, an edge not aligned. I pry it loose, revealing a photo taped behind it.

Three men. Declan, younger Jack, and a third man with his face partially obscured by fire damage. His posture is rigid. The angle staged.

Jack steps beside me. "That was our last covert op together. I remember the location… but not the photographer. Or that man."

"Could that be Thorne?"

He hesitates. "Could be. But if it is, we're already deeper than I thought. Thorne was never meant to be on the record."

We take everything we can carry. Jack grabs a half-melted thumb drive and a scorched notebook from under the shelf; whatever survived the burn. We don't stop to read, just stuff it into the pack and move.

As we step out, Jack pauses at the edge of the front path. His hand shoots out, grabbing my arm and pulling me back toward him before I take another step.

"Wait," he says, voice low in my ear.

He crouches slightly, eyes sweeping the path. Then he sees it, the nearly invisible filament strung low across the threshold, stretched taut between a cracked post and a rock half-buried in the dirt. We were lucky not to trigger it on the way in. Somehow we must've stepped just high enough to clear it without realizing. It's a professional setup, precise and nearly invisible.

"Tripwire," he mutters.

Before I move, he shifts closer, one hand bracing against my back, the other around my arm, drawing me close until I'm flush against him, the warmth of his chest pressing into my back. We stay like that for half a breath; tension held between us like the wire itself.

Then he eases back and gestures behind him. "We need to move. Now. Someone's watching this place. We're not the only ones looking for Thorne."

We retreat fast and quiet, with no time to look back. Not yet.

When we get to the truck, I don't speak until we're a good ten miles out, and even then, it's just a glance at Jack's grip on the wheel. His hands are tight, his knuckles pale, and he hasn't blinked much since we pulled away. He's running mental recon, I can tell he is replaying every step, every shadow.

"You think it was a kill switch?" I ask quietly.

He shakes his head. "More like a warning. That place was watched, but whoever strung that wire didn't want to make a scene. They wanted to know who came sniffing."

"And now they do?"

Jack doesn't answer. He doesn't have to. The silence is answer enough.

We drive the rest of the way with one eye on the road and the other in the mirrors. By the time we reach the edge of familiar country, my jaw aches from how tightly I've been clenching it.

But even with all that tension, despite the threat, the unanswered questions, there's a strange calm between us. We made it out together. And that means something.

Something that's growing.

Because now we know that Thorne wasn't a ghost. He was real.

And someone doesn't want him found.

Chapter 9

Words on Paper

ELENA

Two mornings later, the ranch feels quieter than usual. Not peaceful. Just still. Jack is out feeding the cattle in the valley west of the ranch house, having spent most of yesterday in the saddle, checking fences and trailing a wayward calf that broke through the south line. He prefers to ranch on horseback, says it's quieter, more honest work. Watching him ride is like seeing instinct in motion. He is steady, sure, and balanced; like the man was born with reins in his hands.

He and Declan grew up like wild country boys on the western slope of Colorado, riding bareback through overgrown fields, swimming in creeks, and chasing chickens just to stir up trouble. Jack once told me they used to tie ropes to tree limbs and swing into the river, no helmets, and no plan. It was the kind of freedom kids don't get anymore. Before things with Declan got strange, I would catch glimpses of the boys they used to be, before secrets fell between them. Before secrets fell between all of us.

After watching Jack disappear beyond the hill, I go inside and sit at the table with the box of Declan's personal effects spread out like a puzzle I should've solved years ago. It still feels like pieces are missing.

Earlier this spring, during the auction in town, a steer broke loose in the middle of the arena. Chaos followed. There were kids scattering, vendors yelling, and me right in the path of a full-grown steer that wasn't in the mood to be corralled. I hadn't seen Jack arrive that day. I hadn't known he was there. But he moved fast, swinging onto a nearby horse without hesitation, guiding it straight into the fray.

One minute, I was standing my ground, frozen like a fool, and the next, Jack was there, sweeping me up and onto the saddle in one fluid motion. Like some rescue seen from an old western movie.

I'd been mad, humiliated even. I didn't want to see him. Didn't want to owe him. But later, when I replayed it in my mind, I realized something cracked open in that moment. The ice I'd built around myself started to splinter. He didn't just save me. He saw me. And didn't hesitate.

That moment, being yanked out of danger, the adrenaline, and the silence after, was the first time I let myself admit there was more buried in me than grief. It cracked something open, not just between us, but inside me. I started letting myself think about Declan. Not the perfect version I'd clung to, but the real man. The secrets. The shadows I didn't want to look at.

Jack didn't ask for that. He just made space for it. And maybe that was the real rescue; giving me the space to finally face the man I married, not just mourn him. To stop protecting the version of Declan I wanted to believe in and start seeing the truth that had been there all along.

This time, I go through everything with intention. Not just grief. Not just nostalgia. I'm hunting.

Near the bottom of a stack of his journals, mostly filled with mundane observations and field notes, I find a letter. Folded into quarters. No envelope. My name written in Declan's familiar, squared-off handwriting.

I hesitate. Then I open it.

The words are messy in places, scratched out and rewritten like he'd drafted it during a storm of second-guessing. It's not dated. Not signed. But it's him.

Unmistakably Declan.

'El,

If you're reading this, then I didn't get the chance to explain. I wanted to tell you everything, but I couldn't, not without putting you in the same danger I find myself in. There's a name, Isaac Voss. If he resurfaces, don't trust what they say. Don't trust the system. Some threats wear credentials."

My breath catches. I read it twice, three times, hoping more will appear between the lines.

Jack walks in just as I'm folding it up. I slide it across the table. He reads it in silence.

"Where did you find it?"

"These journals were part of his personal effects returned to me after his death. I never had the heart to go through them, or the need to. Until now."

He starts to thumb through the stack, then pulls something from a journal that I'd missed. A photo that is tucked between two pages of one of the smaller journals. It's grainy, surveillance style, stamped with time and date. The man in the frame stands in front of a government building. Isaac Voss. Confirmed.

"The date," Jack says. "That's three days before Declan died."

My hands clench in my lap. "I've heard that name before. A long time ago, right before you pulled me out of that mess in Dubrovnik. I didn't know who he was then. Just a whisper in a file."

We're both quiet.

Then Jack says what we're both thinking. "Voss isn't just a piece of Declan's past. He's the link."

I nod slowly. "To the Black Ledger. To T-6. To me. To you."

Outside, the wind picks up again, sweeping across the wheatfields until the golden stalks bend low in surrender, their whispering hush like secrets carried on the breeze. The cattle, sensing something in the air, have begun to cluster near the fence line, noses lifted, bodies close. Even the chickens have taken to the coop early tonight, their restless clucks fading into uneasy quiet. Leaves rustle in the cottonwoods, shifting like something unseen moving just out of sight, just beyond knowing.

There's a tension in the stillness that follows, the kind that prickles along the skin and makes you look twice at the shadows. We're not chasing shadows anymore. Now we're chasing names.

And Voss just became the one we have to find first.

Chapter 10

Breadcrumbs in the Desert

JACK

Some contacts are better left alone. Rafe was one of them.

Rafe Santiago had once been a field operative with deep access to black-market comms; part spook, part survivalist, and entirely self-serving. He didn't take sides; he sold them. I'd first met him during a joint intel-gathering op in Ankara. He'd passed off doctored information to a Russian sub-handler that nearly got three of our guys killed.

51

Declan vouched for him once, calling him 'the shadow broker with nine lives.' And Rafe lived up to it. Every time someone wrote him off, he resurfaced with just enough leverage to stay relevant.

He wasn't a traitor, not exactly, but his loyalties had a price. I've only ever trusted him to look out for himself.

But desperate times don't lend themselves to clean options.

It's late morning when I bring it up to Elena. She's sorting through Declan's digitized files again, double-checking connections we might've missed, and I'm staring at the encrypted notes we pulled from the safehouse.

"I've got one more lead," I tell her. "Off-book. Dangerous."

She looks up. "How dangerous?"

"Rafe dangerous."

She pauses, then nods. "You trust him?"

"No. But he might know where Voss is, or who's protecting him."

We make a plan. She helps me prepare a burner comm backup and checks the satellite map while I pack: a full clip, backup magazine, concealed knife, and a sidearm I trusted more than most men. No tech I wasn't willing to burn or willing to leave behind.

"I'm going with you," she says, cutting through the silence.

I pause; one foot already headed toward the door. "Elena..."

"No." Her voice is calm but unshakable. "We said we'd stop splitting up. We're stronger together. Safer."

I study her for a second. She's not just saying it, she means it. There's no fear in her eyes, just resolve. It pulls at something deep in my chest.

"You know this could go sideways fast."

"I know," she says, stepping closer. "But I won't sit here and wait to see if you make it back. Not again. And I won't be alone out here if someone comes looking."

I nod slowly. "Then we go together."

We load up, both armed and quiet, tension riding shotgun as we pull out down the long road that winds from the middle of the property. The hill we built the ranch house on gives us a wide view of every fence line, pasture, and hollow where trouble could hide. The perch provides a second sight line.

After the last few storms, the road's more washout than gravel, every rut a jolt to the spine. I ease the truck over one particularly deep groove and glance at Elena. "At least the natural speed bumps might slow down any uninvited guests," I mutter.

She huffs a breath of a laugh, not quite amused, but willing to let the tension bleed out for a moment. "Yeah, unless they've got shocks better than ours." Elena's sharper than I've seen in days. She is more focused, composed, eyes scanning the horizon like she's flipping through mental files.

The drive to the coordinates Rafe sends takes us past dust-choked roads and miles of open scrub. It's a part of the state that feels more rumor than place, somewhere maps forget on purpose.

We park the truck half a mile off and make the rest of the approach on foot. Elena watches the ridgelines like a soldier, and for a moment, I remember what she used to do for a living, and how little she's ever really left it behind.

We spot the rusty hangar first. Rafe's already there, leaning against the frame like he owns the forgotten landscape. Arms crossed. Chewing a toothpick like this is just another routine drop.

"You brought heat?" he asks.

"Always," I answer, with Elena flanking me just behind and to the left.

He tosses me a battered notebook. "That's your breadcrumb. Voss went dark, but someone kept funding movement. You find the money, you find the ghost."

But before I can flip it open, something shifts. A glint from the ridge.

Sniper.

"Down!" I bark, lunging for Elena and wrapping my arms around her in a full-body tackle. I hit the ground first absorbing the brunt of the impact, Elena landing on my chest behind a stack of crates just as the first shot cracks overhead, the impact has enough force to jolt the air from my lungs. A round punches through Rafe's shoulder before he can move.

Chaos erupts. Return fire from a second location. This isn't just a warning, it's a shutdown.

We don't wait. I secure the notebook. Elena covers us with a clean sweep of return fire, and we move. Fast, low, cutting across the gravel to the left side of the hangar where a rusted service door hangs loose on its hinges. The ridge above gives the sniper a dominant view, and we're exposed the moment we break cover.

I yank Elena down behind a row of concrete footings, bullets biting into the dust inches from us.

"We have to loop wide!" she shouts, already pivoting to cover our next dash. I nod, jaw tight, and sprint low along the line of abandoned fuel drums while she keeps the fire on the ridge suppressed.

We make it to the tree line, hearts hammering. Rafe doesn't move from where he fell, his body fades into the dust and distance.

We don't look back.

By the time we get back to the ranch house, my shoulder's screaming but Elena's got a gash on her forearm from a ricochet, but we're breathing. That's more than I can say for Rafe.

I set the first aid kit on the table beside Elena and gently clean the scrape on her arm before wrapping it with a fresh bandage. It's not deep and thankfully nothing that will need a doctor.

As I return the kit to the cabinet, a sharp pulling in my shoulder makes me flinch. The fall hit me harder than I thought.

Elena's eyes follow every movement. "You're hurt," she says, her voice low but steady.

"I'll live." I hand her the notebook. "Rafe died for this."

She doesn't flinch. We sit down and get to work.

The pages are filled with ciphered notes; layers of code nested into dates and locations. Elena's faster than I expect, sliding into the rhythm of decryption like it's second nature.

"There," she says, pointing. "A list of names. M. Thorne. S. Carlisle."

My brow furrows. "Thorne we expected. Who's Carlisle?"

Elena goes still. "Sam."

She says it like it's an answer. Like it unravels something she doesn't want to admit.

I wait, watching her.

She barely whispers, "Why would he be on a list like this?"

Chapter 11

As a Team

ELENA

We don't say it aloud, but something shifts after Rafe. Jack doesn't retreat behind his silence like he used to. And I don't hold my questions quite so close to the chest.

We sit side by side at the table now, not just because it's easier to work that way, but because it feels right. We're not shielding each other anymore. Not from the weight of what Declan left behind, not from the truth that's rising fast to meet us.

57

The notebook Rafe gave his life for is full of fragmented trails; names, numbers, coordinates scratched in shorthand. Jack lays out the pages while I track the ciphers back through Declan's archived files. Now and then, our shoulders bump as we lean in over the same line of text, neither of us pulling away.

At one point, Jack lets out a slow exhale and leans back. "We need air." He doesn't look at me when he says it, but his voice is low and almost hesitant, like there's more behind the words then needing a break.

We step outside, blinking into the pale mid-morning light. Nugget, our most ill-tempered hen, is waging a one-bird war against the feed bucket. She knocks it over triumphantly and then proceeds to chase two other hens across the yard.

Jack chuckles. "Future queen of the barnyard indeed."

"She's definitely the muscle," I reply with a sly grin.

We stand in silence for a beat, then Jack jerks his chin toward the path behind the coop. "Walk?"

I nod.

We follow the narrow trail that winds through the sloping pasture behind the shed, up toward the old cottonwood tree Jack once called "the perch." I didn't make it this far that night during the ambush in spring, but I remember moving along this very path; heart pounding, breath held, scanning for shadows and enemy shapes. It looks different now. In daylight. With no gunfire. And with a good-looking rancher beside me instead of radio silence and panic.

The perch overlooks most of the hundred-acre spread, and from here, you can see the distant ridgelines that frame the property. Storm runoff has carved new grooves into the earth, but the grass is starting to grow back. In the distance the Rocky Mountains rise on the western horizon, blue sky above.

We sit on a homemade bench, our knees barely touching. He doesn't speak right away. Neither do I.

"I used to come up here when Declan and I were figuring out how to fence this place," Jack finally says. "We were still remembering how to run cattle then. Just knew we wanted to return to something quiet."

Down in the valley, the herd has gathered near the creek. The recent storms left the lowland lush and green, and the cattle have settled in comfortably, chewing slow and lazy like they know they've got the best spot on the ranch. The peace they embody makes his words land even heavier.

"You did," I murmur, glancing out over the valley. "It's quiet, and strong… like it remembers who it was built for."

I turn my head just slightly and catch him watching me. Our eyes lock, just for a second. Long enough for something unsaid to pass between us. Then Jack shifts his gaze back to the ridgeline, like looking too long might give something away neither of us is ready to name.

-"We didn't expect it to last. Peace, I mean. But we had plans, Declan and me. Bigger than cattle. We talked about building something more permanent out here. A retreat, maybe. A place for guys like us to land when they came home with more ghosts than medals. He called it 'the reset button.' Said we'd build cabins along the tree line and teach horsemanship and cattle ranching to men who'd forgotten how to breathe without checking their six."

His voice gets caught between memory and regret. "It sounds crazy now, but back then it felt like the only kind of future worth aiming for. He started with this bench." He pats the slats fondly, "He wanted to create a walking trail from the cabins to the perch, then down along the valley and back up. Install physical training stations every half mile to allow the body to process as much as the mind."

I nod, the breeze tugging a few strands of my hair loose. "He mentioned it to me once, not in full detail, but the idea of a place for healing. I thought it was a fantasy, honestly. Something he needed more than he knew how to build. But hearing it from you... it makes sense. It sounds like him; peace, I mean. But I think Declan hoped... hoped someone would come along and make it mean more."

I let the wind fill the silence for a while before I speak, "One set of coordinates keeps showing up. A decommissioned comms facility in the southwest, near Four Corners."

Jack turns his head slightly, "I know it."

I glance at him curiously. "You've been there?"

He nods, eyes distant. "Once. With Declan. We were just doing recon, but even then something felt off. Place was too quiet for a site that was supposed to be shut down."

I study him. "You think it ties into this?"

"If it's connected to Thorne, Voss, or T-6..." His voice trails off, before looking at me. "It might be where it all started."

I straighten. "Then we go."

Jack's jaw tightens, but his voice is steady. "Together. No ghosts between us this time." I glance at him, caught off guard by the softness in his tone.

"You okay?" I ask.

He holds my gaze. "Yeah. Just realizing... I don't see you as someone I have to protect anymore." My brows lift, the words sinking in like heat against a cold place inside me. "I see you as my equal," he adds.

I don't speak. Just reach over and let my fingers brush his before rising to my feet. But inside, something shifts.

Grief hasn't vanished. But in its place, there's something steadier. Shared purpose. Forward motion.

We're not just following Declan's trail anymore.

We're tracking T-6.

Together.

There's something special about that.

Chapter 12

Red Lights

JACK

The road to the old comms facility hasn't been driven recently. The last time I was here, Declan was driving. We were both running on two hours of sleep and bad coffee, chasing rumors through cut-off channels. It was the kind of job where nothing was official, and everything had shadows. We didn't talk much, just kept our eyes open and our weapons close. That was before everything fell apart. Back when T-6 was just another code.

Now, the brush is thick, the tracks mostly swallowed by time. Elena sits beside me; eyes scanning the horizon, hand resting lightly near the gearshift. It's early, the sun still climbing, and the light cuts through the dust like gold.

The building itself rises like a memory that is half-buried in sage and shadow. It's smaller than I remember, but the reinforced doors and rusted out sensor mounts still tell the story of what it used to be. Not quite abandoned. Not quite forgotten.

We circle wide before approaching. Check for tripwires. Movement. Nothing.

Inside, the air smells like heat, old wiring, and silence. The front rooms are empty, most of the gear stripped years ago. But deeper in the belly of the place, past a set of steel doors that groan on their hinges, we find it: a broken-down comms board, half-covered in dust, tucked behind what used to be an equipment rack. It's recessed into the wall, like it was meant to be hidden. I brush away the debris and check for power fully expecting nothing.

But the machine powers on.

Elena wipes off the console. The screen flickers.

"Looks like the archive directory's been wiped," she murmurs, tapping through layers. "But not overwritten. There's still trace data."

That's when we find it, the mention of T-6. Not a person, but a rotating field designation. A code passed from one deep-cover asset to the next.

She leans forward. "This one... it was last assigned to an operative code-named S. Carlisle."

My stomach knots.

Elena's quiet for a long moment, and then she speaks; slow, like dredging up from deep water. "I saw that name once. On a roster. A classified op I brushed up against years ago. I didn't know who he was back then. Just a name that stuck."

We both fall silent.

Sam's not just someone Declan crossed paths with. He's active. Current. But as the silence stretches, I can't help remembering how he found me before the ambush, not the other way around. He recognized Elena that night, too. Not just in passing. Like he'd been keeping tabs or carrying something heavier than orders.

If he meant harm, he had his chances. Maybe this code name, S. Carlisle, doesn't mean he's the enemy. Maybe he's buried in the same mess Declan was trying to untangle.

Current. Which means he could be the reason Declan never made it out.

Elena glances toward the ceiling, frowning. "Hear that?" she whispers. It's faint, like a hum buried behind the walls, mechanical and intermittent, too rhythmic to be background noise. I tilt my head, catching it just before it fades.

"Could be a relay or sensor cycling. Maybe dormant tech waking up," I murmur. But it's enough to raise our suspicions. We exchange a look, neither of us says the word 'surveillance,' but it's in the air between us; coiled and waiting.

We back out of the room slowly, taking photos of the logs, making sure not to disturb anything else. Outside, the wind has picked up.

Elena steps forward and pauses, "We're being watched."

I follow her line of sight, but I see nothing. Still, I trust her instinct. We climb back into the truck and head out fast, dust curling behind us.

Chapter 13

Also Known As

ELENA

It took us a few days to track Sam down again and set the meeting. Even with what we'd discovered, reaching someone buried that deep in the system meant patience, and just enough persistence to raise a flag without triggering alarms.

In the meantime, we cross-referenced everything we had. Notes, maps, voice memos, turning the kitchen into a full-scale ops board. When the walls started closing in, we took a break the only way we knew how. We turned to nature and hiked the Incline in Manitou Springs; two thousand steps straight up the mountainside.

Jack said it was to clear our heads, but I think we both needed to remember what it feels like to fight for something and be rewarded with a view that reminded us of the world that is still out there.

We both reach the summit breathless; soaked in sweat, and silent as we take in the view. Below, the city of Colorado Springs faded into open plains; gold and amber waves. Above, the sky stretched wide and quiet in every shade of blue you can think of.

Other climbers are working their way up the Incline. Some stepped off to the sides taking a breath, some cheering on their friends, and some sitting where they stop. Jack and I had made it rather quickly considering, but it felt good to take on the challenge, one step at a time.

"I forgot how big the world feels from up here," I said, still catching my breath. "Like... everything bad falls behind you on the climb."

"You and Declan hiked this once," Jack said, his voice low.

I nodded. "He pushed the pace. I hated every step... until I saw this view. Same as now."

"You don't have to forget him to make room for something new."

I turned to look at him, not sure I should say it, but I do anyway. "I know. But it still surprises me who I want that room to be for."

For a second, he doesn't move. Just holds my gaze like he is trying to make sense of something he hasn't let himself hope for. His hand comes to my face, slowly and carefully, and he tucks a strand of hair behind my ear.

No words. Just that small, deliberate touch.

And it says everything.

We set the meeting with Sam under the cover of dusk, neutral ground in a canyon cut through scrubland and wind. Jack insisted on choosing the location. Narrow access points. Good visibility. High ground if things went south.

It was classic Jack. Controlled risk. Contingencies baked into every angle.

We arrived three hours early. Jack scans the ridge. I stay quiet, watching the sky dim with a soldier's caution I hadn't used in years.

When Sam showed up alone, hands visible, no weapon drawn, somehow it felt wrong. Not dangerous, exactly. Just... unexpected. He moved like someone who knew the rules of a meeting but didn't intend to play by them.

The second I saw his face again, something inside me bristled. A flicker of memory, sharp and unfinished. Like smoke curling from a fire I couldn't see. But he looked at me like he *knew*.

"Been a long time," Sam said easily, eyes landing on mine. "Or should I say... Riley."

That name landed like a punch to the chest. My muscles tensed. Jack didn't know it, not really, not what it meant, not how deep it ran.

"You remember that night in Rijeka?" Sam continued, tone casual but eyes sharp. "You vanished before the dust even settled. I figured someone had you burned or buried. Didn't expect to see you again, especially not with Declan, or now Jack."

"Why were you there?" I asked, voice low.

"Same reason as you," he said. "I was embedded. Deep. You almost blew my cover."

"You used me," I snapped.

"I protected you, Riley," Sam countered, too calm. "In the only way I could. You weren't ready to know what was really going on."

That name.

I hadn't used it in years. Not since the op that blew sideways. Not since the orphanage fire.

Jack stiffens; his stance changes, body angled to intercept as he steps closer to me. Just slightly, but enough that I felt the shift— like a silent barrier had gone up between us and Sam. His hand hovers near the small of my back, not touching, just there. Protective and steady.

"Careful," his voice low, eyes locked on Sam. Then, his voice sharpened. "Why'd it surprise you? Seeing her with me?"

Sam raised both hands half a step higher, like he wasn't there to fight. "Easy. No threat. I came alone."

Jack doesn't relax.

"We read the logs," I said. "T-6. S. Carlisle. You've been part of this longer than you've let on."

Sam's smile didn't reach his eyes. "I was never supposed to be found. That's the job. But now that you have..." He shrugged. "You're looking in the wrong direction."

"What does that mean?" Jack asked, voice tight.

Before he can answer, a low hum fills the air, barely audible at first. Then growing.

Drone.

Sam's eyes narrowed. "You led them here?"

Jack shook his head. "We weren't followed."

"Doesn't matter." Sam's voice sharpened. "Move. Now."

The first sweep of the drone came fast; low and silent until it was directly overhead. A thin red beam cuts across the rocks, pausing for half a second where Sam had just been. Not a spotlight. A targeting laser. Whoever was piloting that drone wasn't just watching; they were ready to fire.

The three of us scatter. Jack grabbed my arm and pulled us behind a boulder. Sam breaks the other way, disappearing into the scrub and rock.

"Backtrack to the truck," Jack barks. "Cover low. Move fast." We moved in coordinated silence, weaving through brush, the whine of the drone cutting like a blade through the canyon air. One shot hit close. Too close. Dirt sprays up beside my leg.

By the time we make it to the truck, there is no sign of Sam.

Gone like smoke.

Neither of us said much on the drive home. Both of us glancing in the mirrors, counting shapes in the landscape, hearts still racing from the run.

I sit on the porch with my arms wrapped tight around my ribs, the sun dipping below the Rockies and throwing long shadows across the plains where the cattle graze; unaware of the threat that had just swept over Jack and me.

Jack paces near the perimeter of the house, his boots crunching softly over the gravel paths as he makes a slow circle. To most he would look like he is just stretching his legs, but he is checking angles, sightlines, entry points, and perimeter alarms. Watching the tree line. Listening for the unnatural whir of rotors. Every few minutes, his eyes cut toward the road, then to me. Watching. Measuring.

Tonight he had closed the gate at the road and placed a lock on it. It wouldn't keep people out, but it would slow them down.

When he finally sits beside me, the porch swing creaks under his weight.

"I think Sam knows what happened to me," I say softly, my gaze locked on the hills. "Maybe more than I ever let you know."

Chapter 14

Misdirection

JACK

We should've moved after the drone. After the flash drive. After the safehouse. Instead, we kept waiting for the next clue, the next breadcrumb to make sense of everything Declan left behind. But something had shifted; we weren't chasing shadows anymore. We were standing in the crosshairs.

Elena didn't say it outright, but I saw it in the way she paced. How she barely touched her coffee. The tension in her shoulders, like her skin didn't quite fit. The way she flinched, just slightly, whenever the wind shifted or a bird landed too hard on the tin roof.

She wasn't spiraling, but something was breaking loose inside her. I could feel it. The way she lingered near the doorframes, listening longer than necessary. How she double-checked the locks she'd already checked. How she kept brushing the inside of her wrist, like she expected to find something missing there.

When she finally sits on the porch swing, I wait.

She doesn't speak right away. Her knees are pulled up, eyes fixed on the horizon, where dusk bleeds across the sky. I know that look. She's not seeing the mountains. She's seeing something buried.

"It was Rijeka," she says quietly. "They called it an orphanage, but it wasn't." I stay quiet, leaning against the post, giving her room. "Kids were there, but they were just a front. The place moved information. People. Things no one wanted traced. I was Riley then. Deep cover. Not even my blood type matched the paperwork." She lets out a short, dry laugh.

"When it went south, they didn't try to hide it, they just torched the place. Accelerants in the vents. I was trying to pull out two kids. Got caught in it."

She rubs her forearm absently, as if the fire's still there.

"Someone pulled me out. I never saw his face. Just a voice, steady and calm saying, 'You're not dying here today.' Then nothing."

She traces invisible circles on her jeans with her fingers, her eyes far away.

"It wasn't until I saw Sam's face at the ranch that something… clicked. Not fully. Just a flash. The way he moved. The way he watched, quiet, like everything was a calculation." She pauses. "Maybe it's nothing. Maybe it's him. I don't know."

She doesn't mention the other person she suspects. She doesn't have to. I've learned to read what she doesn't say.

"I woke up in a clinic in France. New chart. New name. Riley didn't survive that fire. After that, they pulled me into intel, quiet stuff. Drops, decoys, dead-letter flags. No more embedded work. Too many risks."

I nod slowly. "And you let them believe Riley died."

"She did," she says simply. "At least the version they trained."

I move to sit beside her, hand resting on her knee. She doesn't flinch.

"Would you want to know?" I ask. "If it really was Sam?"

She takes a long moment to consider it, "Only if it changes something."

There's weight in her voice, like she's lived with unanswered questions for years and learned to carry them. Whatever name she wore, whatever fire she walked through, I know who she is now.

And I'm not letting her walk through the next one alone.

The cold glow of the laptop at the kitchen table casts shadows around me as Sam's warning taunts me, '*You're looking in the wrong direction*' keeps looping in my head.

I run it against every coordinate, every line of Declan's notes, every number in Rafe's pocketbook. Nothing adds up. It all loops back to Declan. To Voss. And now to Elena.

She's across from me, one leg tucked under her, flipping a pen through her fingers like a nervous tic. I watch the curve of her shoulder in the lamplight, the quiet furrow in her brow, the way she holds silence like it's safer than words.

There's something unguarded in me now. A softness I didn't expect. I should've told her more when we met. I should've given her truth instead of half-truths and deflections. But honesty then would've meant unraveling everything I was holding together.

When she met Declan, it happened fast. Too fast maybe, but not surprising. She would drop by the ranch like she was trying not to get attached: muffins, grazing permits, a question about calves. Declan saw through that. He reeled her in, steady and confident. He had the kind of calm that felt unshakable. Within weeks, she was staying overnight. Within months, they were married.

I told myself it made sense. He needed steady. She needed safety. And I kept my distance. Because what I felt didn't belong anymore.

She hasn't spoken in over an hour when her voice, barely a whisper, startles me. "I think I passed intel to Sam. Back in Rijeka." I look up. "I didn't know it at the time. Just... a soft voice. Calm. I thought he was a contact. Never saw a badge. Never got a name. But tonight, something in his voice triggered the memory."

The words fall between us like a detonation. Before I can respond, the perimeter alarm chirped: short and sharp. For half a second, we froze.

I reach under the table for the Glock and move to the window. Elena didn't need instruction. She is already moving to the hallway, grabbing her own sidearm and shoving the papers we had spread out on the table into her go-bag, slinging it over her shoulder after tossing me my own.

My phone buzzes in my back pocket. A number I don't recognize. No contact. Just a message.

MOVE. NOW.

"Elena, back door."

We bolt. Out the side door; we clear the step, I reach back and grab her hand. Not just to guide her through the dark, but to make sure she is still with me, still okay. Her fingers tighten around mine for half a second before we break apart to move faster. It wasn't just a reflex, it was reassurance, a moment of contact in the middle of chaos. And even after she let go, some part of that touch stayed with me, like we'd silently agreed we weren't doing this alone anymore.

We move down the slope behind the shed where the fence had gone soft. Our boots kick up loose gravel and grass as we run low, adrenaline pounding in time with every breath. A figure moves in the tree line behind the barn: shadowed, silent. Too far to identify, but not too far to shoot.

I fire three shots. They duck. We don't wait to see if they recover.

The truck is already backed into the tree line for cover and quick escape. Elena throws open the door, climbs in as I round the front and peel us out, headed east on a route that's not established, but I know the way.

We don't speak until we hit the old gravel road five miles out. Finally, she breaks the silence. "That message... was it Sam?"

I shook my head. "Could've been. Could've been someone else watching him. Watching us."

Her voice was tight. "Jack, if I passed something back then...if they used me..."

"They did," I said. "And maybe Sam was the only one who saw it."

I didn't tell her then, but the fallback cabin we were heading to? I'd never told Declan about it. Never told anyone.

Some secrets are insurance. Some are sanctuary.

This one needed to be both.

Chapter 15

Safe House Truths

ELENA

Jack tells me about the safehouse on the drive in. How not even Declan knew it existed. He had said, "Some things you build for when everything else breaks." His voice was steady, but there was something brittle beneath it, like saying the words aloud cost more than he'd admit.

The two of them had grown up together, joined the military side by side, and made it through selection, through the grind and grit of war. But somewhere toward the end, Declan had slipped out of reach. He had started taking darker assignments, deeper covers. Jack never held it against him, not really. But I think he always wondered what changed. Now, hearing it from Jack, I saw the fracture lines more clearly than I ever had before.

We pass through the concrete maze of the city and exit the other side on dirt roads that twist and turn deep into the Rocky Mountains. As we round the final curve, the headlights bring the small cabin into view, and I catch my breath. Something stirs at the edge of my memory faintly, like a page half-turned. The outline of the structure reminded me of a deed I'd found after Declan died. Folded into an old field manual. No name, no address. Just coordinates and a seal I didn't recognize.

I hadn't thought about it in weeks, maybe longer. But now, seeing this place, something about it scratches at the same corner of my mind. I didn't say anything to Jack. Not yet. I wasn't even sure what it meant. Jack's cabin is tucked low against a ridge, almost swallowed by trees. Weather-worn, shuttered tight, but solid. Built by a man who expected no help and didn't need an audience.

The kind of place you'd go to disappear. The kind of place you trust with your last truth.

Jack doesn't say much as he secures the perimeter. Just methodical motions: bolting shutters, checking sightlines, setting tripwires in the brush.

Before settling in, he crouches near a wall panel and pulls out a metal box from a small, dust-covered nook behind the fireplace. Inside, it's loaded with MREs, vacuum-packed coffee, and iodine tablets. Typical Jack. Prepared, pragmatic, and somehow still thinking about meals. He offers me a packet like it's a peace offering, or just a reminder that we're still human in all this.

I take the MRE packet from him and peer at the label. "Beef stew," I mutter. "If the crackers are stale, I'm revolting."

Jack lets out an actual laugh. Not a snort. Not a huff. A real, surprised, full-throated laugh that cracks the tension in the room like sunlight breaking through clouds.

It makes me smile, and makes something inside me shift. He looks at me a second longer than he should; a smile still lingering on his face. I can feel it now; a quiet acknowledgment between us. Something warm. Something safe. Then the moment passes.

When we are done eating the less than five star meal, he finds me by the small stone fireplace, arms crossed, still trying to calm myself.

"You going to tell me the truth now?" I ask quietly. "About Dubrovnik."

He stops, head lowered. The firelight catches the edge of his jaw. For a moment, I don't think he'll answer. "I wasn't sent to rescue you," he says. "The order was to retrieve a compromised agent. And eliminate liabilities."

My breath catches. "I was the liability."

"You were supposed to be," he says. "But the moment I saw you... you didn't fit. You were lost, yes. Scared. But you weren't dirty. Not like the others. You didn't know what they'd pulled you into."

I sink onto the edge of the cot, staring at the floor. "I didn't. I had no idea."

Jack kneels in front of me. Not close enough to touch. Just close enough. "I made the call," he says. "I got you out, burned the rest. Wrote the report how I needed to. Declan never knew."

I look up, and this time, I see it in his eyes. Not just guilt. Not just regret.

Something else. Something deeper. Our eyes stay locked as the truth settles between us. When he looks away, I somehow feel empty.

Jack stands and unrolls a rubber mat near the fireplace and tosses down a sleeping bag. Clearly he had planned to make do in the safe house on his own and not with a guest. He glances at the makeshift bed, then at me, as if calculating logistics and lines he isn't sure he should cross.

"I can take the floor," he says.

I shake my head. "You won't sleep anyway. And that floor looks like it'll leave bruises. We'll share. Besides…" I nod toward the dimming fire, "if we're both going to freeze tonight, we might as well make use of body heat. Less smoke, less light, less chance of being found."

He hesitates just a beat longer than he needs to. Then nods.

As he moves to adjust the sleeping bag, I watch him. Jack is quiet, thoughtful, and endlessly respectful. He hasn't touched me once without permission, hasn't assumed anything, even in moments where he could have. It makes me wonder what kind of man he really is beneath all the gruff silence, the soldier's instincts, the rancher's frame. Someone who walks like he's used to bearing weight alone; and still makes space for others beside him.

When we lay down, it's side by side on the mat, under the sleeping bag. No words. No promises. Just heat and safety. But I like the feeling of Jack next to me. Solid. Steady. Safe.

Just breath between us. And warmth.

That night, I don't sleep. I drift. And when I do sleep, it's the chickens I dream about; ridiculous, noisy, feathered chaos. Nugget trying to perch on the water bucket. The others flock behind her like she's some barnyard messiah. It makes no sense. And somehow, it's the safest dream I've had in years.

Morning breaks soft. Gray-blue and hushed. Jack's already up, heating water over the stove. He glances over his shoulder when I step out of the room.

"When this is over," he says, "we'll go back to your little army of hens."

I smile, tired but real. "Were you in my head last night?" I ask, nudging his arm lightly. "I dreamt about them. Nugget was ruling the coop like a tiny dictator." Jack huffs, a small smile on his face. "I guess we're in sync," I add. "Or maybe I just miss my chicks."

We sit on the tiny makeshift porch step, boots side by side, knees touching, coffee cooling between us, watching the sun come up in the split of the mountain ridges that overlook the plains. The view is both familiar and surreal.

Colorado Springs spread out in the distance below like a toy city, the open prairie stretching far beyond. Small clusters of buildings blink gold in the morning light, framed by the distant haze of the plains rolling into the horizon. It's strange to be this high up, surrounded by mountains, yet looking down at the rest of the world like we're watching it wake without us.

"There was a man," I say. "Back then. Before it all went wrong. He told me not to go to that final meeting. He didn't say why. Just... warned me."

"You think it was Sam?"

I nod slowly. "The voice. The calm. I think he tried to help then too. Quietly. And I ignored it."

Jack doesn't speak right away. Then he says, "You didn't ignore it. You survived it. That's different."

The air between us settles into something soft, something earned.

He shifts slightly. His arm brushes mine. I don't move.

"You scare me sometimes," I whisper. "In the way I want to trust you." Jack looks over, something unreadable in his eyes. "I'm still here, and I'm not running."

He reaches up and tucks a loose strand of hair behind my ear before I lean into him a little. He doesn't move away. Perhaps I imagine it, but I think he leans in to.

"Elena…" Jack's voice drifts off like he wants to say more, but he stops at my name. I do like the way it sounds when he says it.

The shared weight of everything we've carried, finally feels lighter. It's not just about Declan anymore. It's about what comes next.

It's us. And we're still standing.

Chapter 16

Silence & the View

JACK

We don't talk much on the drive down from the cabin. There's a heaviness between us; not tension, but like the gravity of what we're chasing has started to settle into our bones.

The morning light breaks over the hills as Elena flips through another of Declan's journals. She's been cataloging his notes, searching for patterns. I watch her from the corner of my eye, the way her brow furrows when something clicks.

84

She taps the page with her finger. "Here. *'If they come for me, I'll leave the truth where no one can hear the lies.'*"

I lean over to read the scrawl. My breath stills, "I know where that is."

She looks up, searching my face. "Where?"

"There's an overlook. High up in the San Isabel range. Declan and I used it during our military years, when we needed to breathe or talk without radios or shadows, we went there."

"Someplace off the grid then?"

"Completely. No signal. No drone coverage. If he left something behind… it'd be there." I clench my jaw.

Silence settles between us; I think Elena feels it too. If we're right, it means Declan had been hiding things for a while, long enough to slip back to Colorado during that last mission. He must have made the climb, hiked the ridge, and left something behind. Something he didn't want anyone to find, at least not right away. Another breadcrumb.

We stop in the closest town before heading toward the range. We're both experienced, but neither of us is properly outfitted for a climb. I know the terrain, remembering it too well to let us go unprepared. We need to gear up.

I grab a map, water, protein bars, and a couple hiking poles, just in case. Elena picks out a thermal layer and gloves, eyeing me like she knows I'll comment but doesn't care. I nod instead. It's smart and practical; just like her. We don't say much at checkout, but the weight of what we're doing hangs in the air.

The hike is as rough as I remembered; loose shale, steep switchbacks, and enough silence to make it feel like the trail's watching us. We start in a patchwork of gold and red, aspens and scrub oaks clinging to the last warmth of fall. But as we climb, the colors thin, the air sharpens, and evergreens take over; stoic and unchanging. Higher still, trees give way to rock, and the wind starts to bite.

Halfway up, Elena's pace slows. Not by much, but enough that I glance back. She's flushed from the climb, breathing hard, adjusting her gloves like they've started to itch from the heat trapped under her layers. The thermal she insisted on is doing its job, maybe too well. She doesn't complain, just nods once; like she's silently thanking me for stopping in town.

I keep my pace steady. The terrain is unforgiving, and I don't want to push her too hard. But she doesn't falter. Doesn't ask for breaks. Just keeps going. And it hits me hard just how much grit she carries: quiet, steady, and without bravado.

Even when everything feels uncertain, she makes it feel like we've still got control. Like this isn't about chasing ghosts anymore but facing them. Together.

We don't speak much. Not because there's nothing to say, but because everything already has weight. I used to think control came from tactics. From readiness. But sometimes it looks like her; bruised, focused, still choosing forward.

When we reach the overlook, I stop short. It hasn't changed. A weathered bench, nearly swallowed by brush, still stands against the drop-off. The valley stretches below, layered in pine and fog.

Elena sets her hands on her hips. "This the place?"

I nod, walking to the bench. After pulling the overgrowth back, I run my hand along the underside, knocking gently until I catch a shift in tone; a dull thud, different from the rest. Hollow.

I reach under and knock again, fingers brushing the uneven slats. One of them gives a little, just enough to catch. I grip it and tug.

The board comes loose with a creak, my hand entering a hollowed-out space, clearly carved with more effort than finesse. I huff a quiet laugh. Declan must've put his high school wood shop skills to use, at ten thousand feet.

Tucked inside, where no one would have ever thought to check, is a small waterproof case, duct-taped into the recess with enough layers to make me roll my eyes. My heart stutters.

I set it on the bench between Elena and I, offering her the opportunity to crack it open.

She looks at me for a minute, her blue eyes hesitant, but holding mine. Quietly she picks up the case. She holds it like it might combust, but then she starts to open it, and she gasps.

Inside: a thick, weathered ledger. Handwritten. Real. Similar to the one we had at the ranch house but worn in ways that suggest Declan kept it close.

No encryption. No passwords. Just truth.

We flip through the pages. Names. Dates. Operations. Voss. Thorne. Dozens of field designations. T-6 appears repeatedly; each tied to untraceable missions.

"Rogue directive," Elena whispers. "This was never meant to be sanctioned."

I nod. "It wasn't. This was off-books. Dangerous. And Declan was documenting it."

Elena turns another page. Then she goes still.

"What is it?"

She swallows. "My initials."

There, in the margin, marked in red: **E.R. - Collateral. Potential leak.**

87

"Even back then, they were watching. I wasn't just caught in Declan's mess. I was part of the file too." Her voice is barely audible. "They tagged me."

I reach over and take the book, closing it as I set it aside. I can feel her shaking beside me, so I pull her close to me and put my arms around her.

"They didn't get you," I say.

"But they tried," she whispers. She leans in then, and I hold her tighter.

We sit in silence, the old bench groaning beneath our weight as the mountain air coils around us. Below, the valley is washed in fog and pine, a place too quiet to lie and too remote to hide. The ledger rests between us, heavy in more ways than one. What we've found could burn everything down or finally bring clarity to what tore Declan apart.

For the first time in days, I don't feel like a ghost chasing ghosts.

We're finally holding the truth.

Chapter 17

Unexpected Alliance

JACK

The drive back from the mountains is long and winding. There are miles of silence, broken only by the hum of tires over cracked asphalt, and the occasional creak of the truck frame shifting with the grade. Elena sits with one hand on the console, her fingers barely brushing mine. Not intentional, but not accidental either; I don't move away.

At one point, she glances over, her voice soft. "I keep thinking about that ledger," she says quietly. "About Thorne. About everything Declan was trying to say before the end."

I nod once, eyes on the road. "He left more than just warnings. He left us a direction." We don't say much more. But her hand stays there. And for a stretch of highway, her pinky hooks around mine.

ELENA

Something's off when we return to the ranch house.

Even before we crest the hill to the house, I can see the animals are restless. The chickens scatter when they usually gather. The horses pacing near the fence line, one tossing their head in agitation. Nugget flaps her wings at shadows that aren't there. Jack narrows his eyes but doesn't say a word. I feel it too; like the land itself is warning us.

The air feels still and heavy.

The tripwire is intact, but the lock on the front door has a scratch that wasn't there before. Inside, nothing's missing, but things have been moved. Jack's pack is zipped differently. The coffee tins label faces the wrong direction. My boots are two inches out of place.

Jack doesn't speak. He just crosses the room, checks the comms, and swears under his breath. "Signal's jammed."

I nod slowly, heart thudding. "Someone's been here."

"I think someone we know."

We look at each other, and we both know exactly who he means. Jack doesn't say the name, but I see it in his eyes: Liam Cray.

A contact from Jack's old unit. The one who'd been feeding intel to Sam from the inside.

Jack grabs the ledger, tucks it into the back of his pants, and silently signals for us to move. But it's already too late.

The first flicker of movement outside the ranch house window is fast. Shadows from the trees. Boots on gravel. Armed men.

We're out the back in seconds, cutting through trees and dodging downhill when a burst of fire rips through the tree line above us.

"Jack!" I call out. It's a plea and a question.

"Keep going, Elena," he says covering me so I can run ahead. I hear him fire shots back toward the house. As I run, the sound gets farther away. Jacks not running, he's engaging.

Suddenly another figure appears through the smoke.

Sam.

He's shouting, waving at me, motioning to a narrow cut in the rock. "This way!"

I don't stop to argue. I run. "Jack!" I say as I get to Sam, "Help Jack!"

"I got him. You run! Follow the natural runoff."

I turn and find the runoff and start to follow. Gunshots, closer this time. I can only hope Sam is on our side.

The trees close in fast, thick with scrubs and hidden stone. I continue to follow the runoff without hesitation. The sound of pursuit fades, and the air thins as I move deeper into the gorge.

I break through a thicket into a dry creek bed. I am breathing hard, scraped up, bleeding in small ways that don't matter. Jack and Sam catch up quickly. Jack looks me up and down assessing for injury. I nod to him, Jack nods back, then turns on Sam.

He shoves him hard. "You sold us out!"

"I didn't!" Sam snaps. "I tried to bait Voss. I tipped Liam. I thought I could trust him. I didn't expect a team." Jack doesn't look convinced. "You think I wanted this?" Sam says. "You think I'd drag her into it if I had a choice?" He looks at me then. Something raw behind his eyes.

"You want the truth?" I say, stepping forward. "Then give me yours. Who was I to you back then?"

Sam exhales slowly. "Rijeka. You were working courier ops, just routine stuff. It was nothing that was flagged for high-risk. But that night, your route shifted. Someone handed you an updated dispatch sheet. It looked official, right?"

I nod slowly, heart starting to thrum. "Last minute change. Said the client was nervous and wanted a quieter drop point."

His jaw tightens. "Wasn't official. That drop point was a setup. The intel leaked through a compromised channel, probably bait to flush out my team."

I go still.

"I was under. Deep. Only knew your name from a passing brief. You weren't supposed to be anywhere near my op. But then you showed up on the perimeter, alone, and you paused. That caught my attention. You didn't go straight in. You hesitated. You even radioed back a time discrepancy. You said the schedule didn't match the confirmation code."

I remember that now. A quick call made to Ops. They brushed it off, told me to proceed.

"You didn't know it, but that moment changed everything," Sam continues. "I was already twitchy, but your hesitation confirmed something was off. So, I broke protocol. Circled wide, went in from the south wall. And you... damn it, Elena, you ran into the fire. For two kids who weren't even part of your assignment."

The air thins around me.

"You were supposed to be a shadow," he says. "But I saw you. Heard you yelling for help inside. I pulled you and the kids out just before the floor collapsed."

My breath hitches. *Smoke. Heat. Panic.* The memory was always fogged or scrambled. But his voice cuts through the dark now like it did then.

"You were out cold," he says gently. "But I stayed close enough to make sure the evac team picked you up. I knew you made it to the hospital. After that... I disappeared. Couldn't risk burning everything. But I kept tabs. Quietly. You didn't know it, but I've been there since. Watching. Trying to protect you from a distance. You weren't my op, but I watched from the edge. Then you married Declan."

I blink. Brows furrowing, mind spinning.

"That's when I backed off," he says. "Figured you were protected. Safe. Declan didn't let many people in, but he let you in. And I figured, for once, someone good landed on her feet." There's a beat of silence before he adds, "I saw Declan in Istanbul. Days before he died."

That pulls me up short. "You what?"

Sam nods. "He looked rough. Like he'd been running too long. He pulled me aside, shoved an envelope into my hand. Told me to get it to Jack when the time was right."

Jack goes still beside me.

"I asked him what that meant by 'the right time,' but he wouldn't say. Just told me I'd know. Honestly? I didn't. I carried that envelope for months, then years, waiting for some sign. Then I heard about the auction house incident. The way you stood there frozen. The way Jack stepped in. The way your name was starting to come up in chatter on the inside; people watching you, asking questions."

I glance at Jack. His jaw is clenched, his knuckles white.

"That's when I knew," Sam says quietly. "Whatever Declan left behind, it wasn't just shadows anymore. It was circling closer. Watching her. Watching both of you. But when I got to the ranch, planning to hand off the envelope to Jack... and saw you standing there?" He shakes his head, voice tightening. "That's when I knew for sure. This wasn't about timing anymore. It was already happening. You were in it, together. And whatever Declan was trying to protect... it was about to land on your doorstep."

I stare at him. "So, you were never just watching *me*."

He shakes his head. "I was watching the storm."

Jack's breathing hard, torn between instinct and choice. I see it in the tightness of his jaw, the way his eyes flick between me and Sam like he's weighing every betrayal against the sliver of truth we just uncovered. Then he looks at me, just for a second, and whatever war he's fighting inside settles. He finally nods once.

"Then help us finish it," he says. "Because next time, we won't get out."

Sam's jaw sets. "Agreed."

Chapter 18

Offers Refused

JACK

Voss. The name circles everything now, like gravity, like rot. Every thread we pull leads back to him. But what we still don't know is the part that keeps me awake: was Declan trying to take him down... or protect him?

The ledger helps. So does Sam.

We hole up at a small rental tucked behind an out-of-season fishing lodge. There are no cameras, no visitors, no questions. It's the kind of place that smells like mildew and old bait, but the locks are sturdy and there's only one road in. I positions the truck under a tarp near the trees, out of view, then board the windows and secure the back door with a wedge I fashioned out of scrap wood. There's a shortwave radio inside, half-broken, but still good enough to pick up military bands when tuned just right.

Sam works from a burner laptop, tracing aliases through private contractors, humanitarian NGOs, and black-budget programs the government won't even admit exist. Elena cross-references documents in the ledger with dates and field codes. We take turns sleeping. No one rests well.

That's when we find it.

A shell company: Pacific Valor Initiative. It appears over and over. On shipments, contractor logs, and even a fake aid organization that ran for six months out of Croatia. Elena goes pale when she sees the name.

"I worked for them. Briefly. Years ago. Thought it was just intake and logistics and refugee aid. But now…" She doesn't need to finish. The silence fills in the rest.

I lean over her shoulder. "You think he was using the front to run ghost ops?"

"Or to build something worse," Sam mutters. "A loyalty chain. No oversight. All command."

Sam leans forward. "Voss pitched me once. Said he was building a new shadow network. Completely off-grid and completely off-record. One chain of command. No oversight. Told me I could be in on the ground floor. I said no."

"And Declan?" I ask.

Sam shrugs. "That's the question, isn't it?"

I pull out my phone, scrubbed and isolated, and play one of the audio clips from Declan. The one we decrypted last week. His voice flickers through static:

"…Voss is already too deep. If I go dark, assume he pulled it. Don't trust anyone who shows up without warning."

The three of us sit in silence. The room feels colder.

Elena gets up and starts pacing. "If Pacific Valor was dirty, and Voss was in charge… Declan must have known. He left that ledger for a reason."

"Elena, that shell company. Would Voss remember you?"

She nods, slow. "Maybe. It was a small team. If he was involved, he probably made a file."

Sam meets my eyes. "Then we've got our way in."

"What are you saying?" she asks.

"We use the ledger," I say slowly. "Leak a hint. Something small enough to draw him out. But it must come from you. If you're visible, if he thinks you're the one holding the truth, he'll come to you."

Elena's eyes darken, but she doesn't hesitate. "I'll do it."

Sam raises an eyebrow. "Just like that?" He looks at her like there's more, but he doesn't say anything else.

She looks between us, fire in her voice. "I've been hunted, lied to, and left behind. If this is the only way to finish it, then yes. Just like that."

I feel something settle in my chest, a direction.

We've drawn the line. Now we wait for the predator to think he's found prey.

ELENA

Later that evening, Jack slips out while Sam runs diagnostics on the signal intercepts. I find him down by the lake behind the fishing lodge, crouched on a narrow wooden dock that juts out into the water. The surface is still and glassy, except where ripples bloom outward from a simple line he's cast. No rod. Just monofilament wound around a stick, an old-school drop line with a weight and a baited hook. It's the kind of method you'd use if you'd learned it as a kid, or from desperation.

He glances over as I approach. "Didn't think you'd follow me."

"I always follow you," I say, and it's only half a joke.

Jack gestures toward the line. "Used to fish like this with Declan. Out past the old cattle line on his family's land. We'd dig worms out of the barn foundation and skip church if it meant a quiet Sunday morning with a canteen and silence."

I sit beside him, knees pulled up, arms wrapped around them. "He used to say you were the quiet one. That if you ever talked, people should listen."

Jack lets out a soft laugh. "He said that to everyone. It made me sound wiser than I was. Truth is, I was just careful with what I said around him. Declan had a way of making you feel like you had to measure your words."

I glance at the hook as it bobs, slow and steady. "He told me once that the three of us would end up on a ranch somewhere, retired and weather worn. You'd run cattle. He'd handle the money. I'd finally get a horse that didn't try to bite."

Jack smiles faintly. "I remember that."

"And then he went and died on us."

The words hang in the air. Neither of us look at each other. "He didn't take everything with him."

I glance at him. "What do you mean?"

He shrugs, but it's not casual. "He left pieces. In you. In me. This fight… it's not just about what he uncovered. It's about what we do with it now."

I nod. "You think we'll come out of this?"

"I don't know," he admits. "But I know this…" He reaches over, lightly brushing his fingers against mine where they rest on the dock. "…we're not doing it alone."

I lace my fingers with his, slow and deliberate. "No. We're not."

We sit there for another minute in the fading light, the sun setting in the distance beyond the western peaks of the Rockies, the line in the water forgotten.

Then Jack pulls in a slow breath. "Tomorrow," he says. "We leak it. One file. One line of truth. And we let it travel."

"And we stay close," I add. "Watch what moves. See who bites."

He nods. "Voss will come for it. He'll want to shut it down."

"And when he does," I whisper, "we make sure he doesn't walk away."

The wind curls around us, sharp with the promise of something coming. Not safety. Not even justice.

But a reckoning.

Chapter 19

To Be Seen

ELENA

The low hum of Jack's laptop, and the occasional scrape of Sam's chair echo through the silence. We're preparing by seeding false leads, layering digital breadcrumbs, and scanning chatter from every dark corner of the web. But it feels like we're holding our breath. Like something is waiting to surface.

It does.

Jack finds it first.

He's digging through the drive again, the one from the ambush, cross-referencing log codes, when he frowns. "There's a hidden partition. It wasn't there before. It must've been encrypted behind a duplicate sector."

He opens the folder. A single file waits inside: **Declan.mp4**.

I don't speak. I just stand beside him as he clicks play.

The screen flickers to life. Declan's face appears. He looks drawn, tired, but unmistakably him. He's in a dim room, somewhere sparse. Maybe a safehouse. Maybe a goodbye. I sit next to Jack.

"If you're seeing this," he starts, "then I didn't make it. And if you have contacted Jack… then I hope you're together." I feel Jack still beside me.

"I found something," Declan continues, voice rough. "Voss isn't just running side ops. He's rewriting the system. Using people, field assets, without their consent. Jack, you were one of them. So was I."

Jack's jaw tightens.

"I marked your name on the map," Declan says, "not because I suspected you, but because I knew you'd be a target. If this blew up, Voss wouldn't leave loose ends. I needed Elena to know who she could trust."

His voice cracks. He swipes a hand across his face.

"Elena… I kept so much from you. Not because I didn't trust you. Because I couldn't protect you and still tell you everything. I was trying to keep the fire from reaching you. I don't know if I did it right. But I tried."

The screen glitches. The file ends.

I sit frozen. Not crying. Not shaking. Just breathing.

Jack reaches over, closes the laptop gently.

I look at both of them then. At Sam, who's been watching quietly. At Jack, who hasn't said a word.

"We finish this. For him. No more waiting," I say, voice firm and unshaking.

And they both nod.

I can't sleep that night. I sit outside on the back porch of the rental, the lake a black mirror stretching behind the pines. The stars looking down like nothing is wrong, like the world hasn't tilted. Jack joins me quietly, settling onto the step beside me.

He doesn't speak right away. Just passes me a mug of reheated coffee before dropping a blanket across my shoulders. "You okay?" he asks.

"No," I answer. "But I will be."

He watches the trees. "Tomorrow changes everything."

"We're going to bring it to light."

He nods, then glances sideways. There's a beat of hesitation, like he's asking permission, even now. Then he exhales and shifts slightly.

"I've been thinking about something," he says quietly. "I wasn't sure if it was right to say it. Not after everything. Not here, not now. But," he swallows, "we've honored Declan tonight. With the truth. With the fight. And I think he'd want us to keep going. Not just with the mission, but with life."

I turn toward him. "What is it?"

"You ever wonder what it would've been like if we'd met first?"

I exhale through my nose. "Sometimes. But then I remember, I wouldn't have been ready for you back then."

"And now?"

I look at him. "Now, I know the cost of being seen. And you... you've never looked away, Jack."

He reaches for my hand. His brown eyes finding mine in a way that I am not sure they have ever been held before, not even by Declan. There is no urgency. Just presence. His thumb brushes the edge of my palm, a grounding gesture. A quiet yes.

In some ways, I feel like there was always a yes for Jack. I loved Declan fiercely, and we were crazy for one another. But there was something about Jack that always called me. This thing growing between us, it's slow, but I am leaning into it.

First though, we have unfinished business.

"Tomorrow, we put out just enough bait," he says. "No more shadows, no more circling. Just enough pressure for Voss to bite."

In the silence that follows, I don't feel afraid.

I feel ready.

Chapter 20

Baited

JACK

We move quickly.

Before we set anything in motion, the three of us gather around the small table in the corner of the rental. I lay out three burner phones, one secure line, a hand-sketched replica of the depot's layout, and a satellite overlay. Sam spreads a topographic map across the surface.

"Two access roads here and here," Sam says, pointing. "They'll block both, which means we need a third exit. Elena, you'll head in from the east. Jack and I will cover the ridge and the old utility platform."

Elena nods. "Sniper nest there?"

"Exactly," I say. "And a fallback trench to the south if it gets hot."

We walk through contingencies, hand signals, blackout windows. The whole plan is crisp, clean, and dangerous, and each one of us knows it.

At one point, I catch Elena's eye across the map. "If comms go dark..."

"Break west," she finishes. "Trench line."

I nod. "And if anything feels off, *anything*, you abort. You don't stay to fight."

"I'm not here to die," she replies. "I'm here to end this." I study Elena for a long moment. Then nod.

We spent the day planning, running scenarios, and looking for loopholes. Now, standing outside alone, the cold brushing against my face as I watch the trees shift under the stars, I hope it's enough. Elena joins me quietly, standing beside me without speaking.

I glance sideways at Elena, her face caught in half-shadow, steady and unreadable as she looks out into the darkness. For a moment, I don't know how to say what I feel. Finally, I speak.

"You've changed." She doesn't answer right away, just watches the night settle in. "You're not the same woman I pulled out of Dubrovnik," I say softly.

"No, I'm not."

I let the silence stretch a beat longer before I continue, "I see you now. Really see you. And it scares the hell out of me."

She turns to look at me, her voice barely above a whisper. "Why does it scare you, Jack?"

I shift slightly, my hands tucked into my jacket pockets, eyes on the trees before I turn to her. "Because when I look at you now, I don't just see the woman I was sent to protect. I see the one I could've lost… and the one I'm not sure I would know how to let go of."

She exhales slowly. Then reaches for me, I reach back for her, her fingers lacing with mine. It's not urgent, just certain. Her voice is quiet. "I'm still here, Jack."

And I squeeze her hand once, not needing words to answer.

Sam interrupts us an hour later. "You're going to want to see this."

He turns his laptop to face us. "Voss's manifest. Charter out of D.C. scheduled for sunrise. Diplomatic shell company. No visible entourage, but the other two listed are former spec-ops, off the grid for years."

My hands become fists. "Rafe mentioned them once," I say. "Voss's private leverage. Not loyal to the flag. Loyal to Voss." Elena looks like her stomach just flipped. I don't move, just mutter, "He's not sending a team. He is the team."

Elena steps forward, my voice low. "Then we give him a reason to show up."

The silence sharpens.

Sam closes the laptop, jaw tight. "If Voss is coming personally, it means he thinks this leak matters. He doesn't leave D.C. for clean-up, he sends others. This time… it's different."

Elena glances between us. "It's a trap for all of us."

"This is our chance," I say. "Not just to catch him. To expose him. To stop this from happening to someone else."

I look at Elena. At the way her hands rest steadily on the table, at the fire behind her eyes. And it hits me again how far she's come. This isn't the woman I pulled out of Dubrovnik. This is a woman standing her ground, choosing to walk into danger instead of run away from it.

"I hate that we're using you as bait," I say quietly.

She meets my gaze without flinching and steps toward me.. "But you trust me to do it."

"I do," I say, the words feel heavier than I expect, because I mean them. Trusting her now means trusting everything that's changed between us, everything we're becoming. I step closer, not rushed, just sure. "We've honored Declan. Now we do the rest."

Elena nods, "Together." She walks away then, calm. Strong. Ready.

I just watch her go, like a man who knows exactly what he's risking.

Outside, dusk bleeds across the sky. A sniper moves into position across the ridge, a shadow figure merging with the tree line.

The trap is set.

Now we wait for Voss to step into it..

Chapter 21

Unexpected Crosshairs

JACK

The next day comes quiet, just sunlight and dust, until Voss's convoy breaks the silence. Two black SUVs tight as a fist, roll slowly into the depot perimeter. Two men step out, smooth, calculated, but my eyes catch on one figure.

David Rourke. My old mentor.

He's grayer now, and heavier in the shoulders, but it's him. He doesn't move like hired muscle. He moves with authority. And he's not here by accident.

Rourke, Declan, and I served together in a dozen shadows no one will admit to. He taught us how to vanish, how to gut intel clean. But he also taught us to question orders; I took that to heart after Ankara. When the bodies suddenly didn't line up with the mission, and the silence that followed spoke louder than any debrief. I walked away. Declan tried to walk away. But Rourke didn't.

I leave Sam in position and loop around behind the staging crates, intercepting Rourke before he reaches the central structure. He clocks me immediately and doesn't draw. Somehow that's worse.

"Didn't think I'd see you again," he says.

"I wish I could say the same."

He lifts a hand. "Let's talk."

We step into the shadowed loading bay. It smells like rust and gun oil; familiar.

"You don't have to do this, Jack," Rourke says. "Let the girl walk. You two disappear. The agency will close your file. No pursuit. Clean slate."

I laugh once, dry. "That's your pitch, Rourke?"

"You've burned enough already," he says. "Don't torch the rest. You do this, you don't come back."

I shake my head. "I stopped coming back a long time ago."

Rourke's face hardens. "Voss is untouchable. This op, or whatever you think you're doing, it won't matter."

I step close. "Then why send you to stop me?"

110

He doesn't answer. I turn and walk away, and I don't look back.

I settle into my vantage point, Elena waiting in the heart of the trap. She is dressed for control. The lines of her clothes simple and sharp, nothing flashy. A pistol at her back, a knife in her boot, and calm in her eyes. Sam watches from his vantage point, rifle trained, comms live.

"He won't hesitate," Sam warns in her earpiece.

"I won't either," she replies.

Voss steps into the depot alone. His suit's too clean for the setting, his walk too assured. But his eyes sweep everything. He knows, or at the very least suspects.

Elena doesn't flinch. She sits at the folding table like it's in a boardroom. A case beside her. The Ledger inside.

Voss stops a few paces away. "Elena," Voss says. "You've gone to a lot of trouble."

She tilts her head, calm and unreadable. "So have you."

A moment passes, then another before he sits across from her.

She brings him up without saying the name, but it's there, woven into her words like a tripwire. And that's when I see it: a flicker. Barely a breath. Voss's mouth tightens. The mask doesn't crack, but it shifts. And that shift is just enough to show there's something beneath it worth hiding.

"Declan chose the wrong hill to die on," Voss says, voice flat.

Elena doesn't look away. "Did he? Or did someone make sure that a field found him?"

Voss leans back slightly, as if he's amused, but his fingers curl tighter around the edge of the table.

And I feel it, like a fault line under the floor. The shift and weight of what's not being said: Declan's name, the envelope, the chatter circling Elena. It's all converging here in this room. Voss is holding the line, but he's not as steady as he wants to be.

He doesn't know what we have. And he doesn't know what Elena remembers.

That's when it clicks. Voss's not here to intimidate. He's here to assess. And if he's nervous, even a little, then we're closer than I thought.

The line between predator and prey is starting to blur. And this time, he doesn't know which side he's on.

I move to a higher perch, old scaffolding above the bay. From here, I've got eyes on Voss and Elena, and a narrow corridor to Rourke, who hasn't left the edge of the depot.

Voss stands and circles the table now, deliberate, hands clasped behind his back like he's teaching a class. "You think this makes you safe?" he asks her. "Dragging out dead men and dead data?"

Elena doesn't bite. She just unlocks the case and turns it so he can see the contents: documents, drives, photographs. The proof that the shadows he played in left bodies. Proof that Declan died for knowing too much.

Voss clicks his tongue. "Declan was sloppy. Got sentimental. That's why he ended up ashes in a field."

Ashes, yeah. That's what the report had said. But even then, I'd wondered why the field was torched. Why no one had questions. Why no one wanted answers. It never added up.

I feel my grip tighten on the stock of my rifle, but Elena doesn't react.

He leans in a little. "You're a lot like him, Elena. Thinking you can fix what was never yours to hold."

She meets his stare evenly. "You're a lot like a man who doesn't realize his time's up."

That earns a slow grin from Voss as he stops and turns toward her. "Cute. But this little show won't change the ending. You'll run. I'll catch up. And Jack?" His voice lifts slightly, like he's pitching to an invisible room, pitching to me. "Jack's still a ghost in the system. I've buried bigger men."

"You talk too much," Elena says. That earns a smirk from me.

He steps closer to Elena, I apply more pressure to the trigger, just enough. Voss leans in low enough for her to hear but barely perceptible through the comms. "Do you know what it costs to erase someone completely? Declan thought he did. That's what made him dangerous. That's what made him disposable."

I key the mic once, a silent signal. Sam murmurs back, "Confirmed. Got your six."

Voss steps back, hands raised. "Fine. You want to play games? Play. I've got back up on every exit. I'm giving you an out. Drop the case. Walk away. Live."

Elena stands slowly. "You're offering deals like you still have the cards."

Voss smiles wider. "I always have the cards."

That's when the first feed from Sam's drone cuts in, there are overlays of movement, signatures. But not ours. Not Voss's men either. Another team.

Another player.

"Jack," Sam says, sharp. "You seeing this?"

"Yeah." My voice is low.

Even Rourke looks up, head tilting as something shifts in the background. It's the last time I see him before he slips out. Whether Rourke ran or was pulled, I don't know. But I doubt he's done watching.

Voss frowns, just slightly. The confident swagger falters. And that's when I know that he's not the only threat.

This just became a three-front war.

And we're right in the middle of it.

Chapter 22

Whispered Truths

ELENA

The silence between us stretches.

Voss doesn't sit. He circles, like a predator about to strike. Measured. Like a man deciding whether to tame a fire or smother it.

I let the moment drag before I reach down and unclip the second smaller case beside me, flip the latches, and open it just far enough for him to see the thick, weathered pages inside.

"It's not a copy," I say. "It's the original. The one Declan kept off the record. The one your people never found."

For the first time, he blinks.

Then the pitch begins.

"Whatever you think this is worth, I can triple it," Voss says. "You want out? Protection? A clean passport, a private estate in Maldives? Done. You want to know the truth? I'll give it to you."

I almost laugh. "You think I want money?"

"I know that everyone wants something."

I lean forward slightly. "What I want is to see the rot and filth ripped out of the system. What I want is for you to answer for what you did to Declan. And what you tried to do to me."

He pauses. Then smiles, but it's tight, shallow. "You were never meant to be involved. You were just... collateral damage." He turns his hand over in the air as if to dismiss me.

I hold his gaze. "And Declan? Was he just collateral too?"

Voss exhales through his nose, slow and deliberate, like he's weighing every word before it leaves his mouth. "Declan got close. Too close," he says, voice tight with something that sounds almost like regret. "He started asking questions, quiet at first, careful, but once he got hold of something, he wouldn't let it go. He kept pulling at that thread, even when it started to unravel everything. I warned him, told him to back off, but you know Declan." Voss pauses, his gaze dropping for a beat. "By the time I realized how deep he was, how far he'd gone... it was already out of my hands. I couldn't contain it quietly anymore. Not without burying him with it."

I stare at him, the taste of bile rising in my throat as I realize what he has just said. "You had him killed."

He doesn't deny it. Just shrugs, as if the weight of what he's saying doesn't register. "He chose his side," he says, voice flat, almost bored. "It wasn't mine." His gaze flicks upward then, sharp, and unflinching, and the silence that follows feels deliberate. It's like a final nail being hammered in. "At least he got a hero's burial."

The smile that spreads across his face after that isn't smug or proud, it's worse. It's cold. Measured. The kind of smile that doesn't belong to someone with a soul. Pure evil, wrapped in a man's skin.

That's when I know. He knew. Back then. Now. All of it.

On the ridge, Sam mutters into comms, his voice low but urgent. "Jack, 3 o'clock; glint off glass."

Jack doesn't answer. He moves.

One shot cracks through the depot air like a lightning strike.

Then the world erupts.

Glass shatters. Metal groans. The sharp echo of gunfire ricochets off the concrete walls, turning the air thick with sound and smoke. I dive behind a rusted-out table as splinters fly, heart slamming in my chest.

Jack bursts through the haze, focused and fast, firing at a second silhouette slipping from the shadows, his aim precise, unrelenting. Somewhere above, Sam's voice barks orders. Short, clipped, military. In the chaos I can't catch the words, only the urgency behind them.

Voss stumbles backward, one arm pressed to his side where dark blood blooms through his shirt. He's wounded but still standing. Eyes scanning. Calculating.

I rise halfway from cover, throat burning, and shout through the chaos, my voice sharp and deliberate. "You should run while you still can, Voss. Because this time, we're not covering it up. We're cutting it out. Every last piece of it."

A beat.

And then, like someone flipped a switch, the gunfire stops.

The air stills. The smoke drifts sideways. The infiltrators vanish. No calls, no retreat signals. Just gone.

Voss's head tilts, and he looks at me from across the ruined depot floor. Blood stains his side, smoke curls behind him, but his voice is steady as he answers.

"You think this ends here?" he calls out, ragged but defiant. "You don't even know how deep it goes."

And with that, he turns and disappears. His form swallowed by shadow and silence.

Jack drops beside me, breath coming fast, scanning me for injury with frantic hands.

"I'm fine," I manage, voice shaking more than I mean it to. "Ledger?"

He gives a short nod, already lifting the hard-shell case from beneath the table. He snaps it shut with a finality that says everything.

We have it.

But nothing about this feels over.

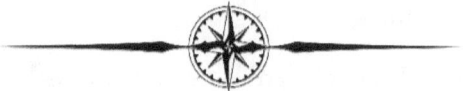

Sam reports it was the Third Front who fired first, then disappeared. No callsigns, no identifiers. Just a few precise shots to light the fuse, then silence. They weren't Voss's. And they sure as hell weren't ours. Just eyes in the dark, pulling strings and watching it burn.

And that concerns me.

But just holding the ledger brings Declan back for a moment. His voice in my ear, the quiet way he'd say my name when he was worried, the way he kept secrets like they were a burden he didn't want to share.

We never knew exactly how Declan died, just that it was an ambush, a failed extraction, and a body burned too badly to question. But I remember the notification. I remember pulling into the ranch, seeing the extra vehicle with military plates. I remember seeing Jack walk out onto the porch, the weight of the world on his shoulders. Right then and there, I fell to my knees in the dirt.

I also remember the way Jack was by my side as the notification team walked me through all the steps and contacts. The silence that swallowed the room, thick and unnatural, like the air itself didn't know how to move. And I remember Jack pacing that night, back and forth across the worn floorboards, muscles clenching so tight I thought he might crack. He didn't cry. Jack never cried. But something about it never sat right with him.

He didn't say much. Not then, not after. Just kept going quiet around the edges, like light fading from the corners of a room. He'd stare off in the middle of conversation, eyes tracking something I couldn't see, or a thought he wouldn't share. When I touched his arm, he flinched. Not like I'd hurt him, but like he'd forgotten I was even there.

The space between us stretched thin and sharp, full of things unsaid. I tried to reach him. God, I tried. But grief like that doesn't leave room for anyone else. He wasn't angry with me. No, Jack was angry with the world, with the way Declan had died, with whatever truths he couldn't prove, and with words left unsaid. And instead of letting me in, he shut me out. He built walls, brick by brick, and called it survival.

And I stood on the other side of that chasm, watching Jack disappear.

Now I know why.

They needed Declan gone, before he could drag the truth into the light. They didn't just cover it up. They buried him with it.

And Jack knew. Maybe not all of it, but enough to feel the fracture before it broke.

Voss was right about one thing.

This isn't over.

Not even close.

Chapter 23

Black, White, & Read All Over

JACK

We don't run. We publish. This is so much bigger than us and we need a team of trusted individuals to help.

Sam and I work side by side in the safehouse cabin still entrenched by the chaos Voss left behind. The smell of spent gunpowder has faded from our clothes, but I can still hear the echo of Elena's voice, steady in the middle of a firefight.

I watched her stand toe-to-toe with a man who orchestrated black ops across three continents, and she never flinched. Not when he offered her a way out, not when he threatened her, not even when she learned he was responsible for her husband's death. Elena stood taller than anyone at that moment. And I knew that whatever came next, she was the kind of woman you didn't protect out of duty. You stood beside her because she let you. Because she was strong enough to carry it all and still leave room for someone else.

I haven't said it. Not out loud. Maybe not even to myself until now. But somewhere between the quiet moments, the storm, and the mess of truth we uncovered, I have started falling for her.

Not with the idea of her, or the woman she was when we first met. Not the one bracing for impact, still fighting shadows she couldn't name. But with the woman she became when everything tried to break her. And the one she's still becoming; steady, unflinching, and finally choosing her own story.

She's more than brave. She's composed under pressure, unshakably resilient, and sharp enough to cut through every layer of deception we've uncovered. What she endured could have broken her. Instead, it honed her into someone who faces the storm head-on. There's a quiet grace in the way she holds herself, and a strength that doesn't ask for permission to exist. She's steel tempered by fire, wrapped in patience, and forged by truth.

Elena sits nearby, hunched over a keyboard, her face lit by the screen. This isn't revenge. It's precision. Strategy.

We leak the first pages of the Black Ledger through whistleblower channels, encrypted and staggered. Operation names. Code markers. Financial routes that lead from "ghost humanitarian aid" to clandestine drone strikes and disappearances that were never meant to be questioned.

The fallout is immediate.

Within forty-eight hours, there are resignations inside three branches of intelligence oversight. Emergency committee sessions convene behind closed doors. And multiple operations listed under Thorne's former directives are "suspended for internal review."

It's not justice. But it's a start.

Elena watches the news cycle spin, the way some outlets call it a conspiracy, the way others run it just above the fold like they're scared to look directly at the sun. She shakes her head, then turns back to her screen.

"I'm writing something," she says.

Her voice is low, but clear. Focused.

When I read it later, it's signed under a pseudonym. Not dramatic. Not explosive. Just a statement. A reckoning.

This isn't about betrayal. It's about memory. About accountability. About the men and women buried beneath orders they never had the right to question.

Sam doesn't say goodbye in person. One morning, I check my phone and there it is:

Debt repaid. Don't look for me.

And I won't. Not yet.

The Ledger is safe. Voss is wounded. His networks are in free fall. But we both know the system that built him doesn't die quietly.

And then there's the third front, the ones that showed up at the depot and then disappeared. Not Voss's men. Not ours. Just... there. I haven't stopped thinking about them since. Sam suspects they were contractors. I think they were something else.

Quiet. Patient. Waiting for the dust to settle before they step out of the shadows.

Because two of the Ledger's dead drops trace back to projects Thorne greenlit years ago, ones we thought were scrubbed clean. Someone else is still out there. Still watching. And they haven't made their move yet.

Elena stands beside me on the porch of the cabin, the wind catching her hair.

"This feels different," she says.

I nod. "It is."

We aren't hiding anymore.

For the first time, the story is ours to tell.

And we're not done yet.

Chapter 24

On the Run

JACK

We moved again, put distance between us and our last location. We holed up in a one-room shack behind an abandoned grain elevator on the western Kansas plains. Dirt floor. No plumbing. A stove that worked when it wanted to. But it was quiet, and for two days, that was enough.

On the third morning, she looks up from her mug of camp coffee and asks, "You think he's gone?"

"Voss?" I shake my head. "No. Men like him don't vanish. They withdraw. Regroup. Delay until the spotlight fades."

She nods like she already knew the answer, then leans forward, elbows on her knees. "So how do we find him before he does that?"

I hesitate because the answer meant risking the quiet we'd carved out. But I opened the laptop anyway. It's an old shell rigged to mimic dead hardware. Sam's last breadcrumb had unlocked a backup routing system tied to ghost accounts Voss had used before. One of them had pinged near Dallas, then dropped off again.

"Elena," I said, "he's not hiding. He's moving. Private airstrip, south of the Texas state line. Shell corporation listed under a medical supply nonprofit."

She sets her mug down. "That's bold. Even for him."

"Means he thinks the walls are still holding. That no one's going to connect the dots fast enough."

"And we're going to prove him wrong." It wasn't a question.

I ran a hand over my jaw, then nodded. "Yeah. We are."

She stands, brushes her hands on her jeans. "Then we intercept him."

"Elena, that's not..."

I stop because I hear it in my own voice. It's too sharp, too automatic. The protector in me flaring up, trying to keep her at a distance from the danger she'd already walked through.

"*That's not your job,*" I was going to say.

Or, "*You've done enough.*"

But that would've been a lie; one built on old habits, not truth.

She cuts in before I can finish. "Don't say it," she said, calm but certain. "Don't say I should stay behind."

I meet her gaze. Unflinching. Fierce. The same look she gave Voss when he called her collateral.

"I wasn't going to," I said finally. "Not this time."

We don't pack light. We pack smart.

Two bags of gear stashed by priority. The ledger. A burner. My sidearm and backup clips. Her knife, a compact Glock, and comms Sam left behind. Extra plates, go bags, burner IDs. Not because we are planning for war, but because we knew better than to expect that it wouldn't come.

She pauses at the door as we leave the safehouse, eyes cast toward the west like she can see all the way back to the ranch. For a moment I see a twinge of regret in those blue eyes, silvered at the edges.

"I didn't even get to say goodbye," she says quietly. "Not to the chickens. Not to Nugget."

I don't have an answer for that because I hadn't said goodbye either. We'd left in chaos, chasing survival.

She shakes her head with a breath that is part laugh, part ache. "She's probably roosting in my boot by now. Or staging a mutiny. Perhaps she even figured out a way to climb up to the ranch sign and peck out a new name for the place instead of True North Ranch."

"We will just have to reclaim the place when we get home," I smile at Elena as I say it.

Then she looks at me. I smile back when she says, "Let's finish this."

I nod. But part of me, selfishly, stupidly, just wants to get her back home. Safe.

We drove most of the night to just south of the Texas-Oklahoma line. Headlights off on the back roads. Just the hum of tires and the occasional flicker of livestock fence lines under the stars. Tumble weeds sporadically blowing across the road.

It is still dark when we reach the edge of the airstrip. But I could feel tension just under the skin. Like something was coming. Like someone already knew we were there.

I park in the shadows of a windbreak and look over at her. She is checking the ka-bar knife I had given her, one hand steady on the leather handle.

"You sure?" I ask.

She looks at me. Really looks.

"I'm not sure about anything," she said. "But I know I don't want to wait for him to come find us."

Now we're here, parked near a private airstrip tucked behind a shuttered grain co-op. Sams tracker found Voss's route south through diplomatic channels, burner credentials, and a ghost's itinerary. He's preparing to leave the country. Possibly for good.

And we can't let him.

I told Elena I'd make the approach alone. We had the entry point mapped, the timing down. But deep down, I knew better.

When I slip through the fence and into the hangar shadows, I catch movement just behind my right shoulder. It's silent, purposeful. Her stride syncs with mine like we've been doing this for years.

I don't need to turn. I know it's her.

"Elena," I murmur.

"We already agreed. I'm not sitting this one out."

There's no heat in it, just resolve. And part of me exhales. Because truthfully, I didn't want to face this without her.

There's steel in her voice. That fire again. It's steady and measured. She's not the woman I once pulled from a bad op. She's more. She's trained, sharp, and here because she chooses to be.

We split without needing to speak. I take the south side, skirting through broken fencing toward the shadows behind a stack of fuel drums. She circles wide along the opposite flank, crouching behind the rusted-out shell of a prop loader. Clean lines of sight. Enough distance for coverage, but close enough to move.

In the hangar, near an old combine, sits a small single engine Cessna. No sign of a pilot; Voss must have someone coming with him, or on the way.

After reconning the area, there is no sign of the third front. Either they've gone underground, or they're waiting for us to do the hard part before they make their move.

I glance across the space and catch Elena's eyes for a moment. She nods. We're ready.

The lone SUV pulls in slower than expected, gravel crunching beneath its tires like an afterthought. When the door opens, Voss' muscle exits first, opening his door. Only one of them, not Rourke, and a small fragile looking man that looks like he was just picked up from a farm. He must be the pilot.

Voss steps out like he's walking into a boardroom. Still crisp. Still smug. But he's off-balance. I can see it in his stance; he is favoring one side. Could be the wound he got at the depot. Could be the realization that this time, he's not in control.

He scans the airstrip casually, then speaks like we're already in mid-conversation. "I told you I still held the cards, Jack."

I step out first. Not fast. Not aggressive. Just enough to let the gravel shift under my boots and draw Voss's eye.

He turns, head tilting like I've walked in wearing a target. And maybe I have.

Elena holds her position. She is quiet, covered; just like we planned.

"Declan was loyal," Voss says, his voice smooth as bourbon. "Until he forgot which side he was on."

I don't respond. I let silence stretch between us like a wire.

He doesn't know Elena's already flanked him and his man. He doesn't know we've mapped every inch of this place for the last few hours. He doesn't know he's already lost.

My fists tighten at my sides. I don't move. Not yet.

Then his gaze shifts, just slightly, like he *feels* her. Not because he sees her, but because he senses the threat that she is.

"He thought he could keep you out of it," Voss says, voice elevating just enough to project to wherever he senses she might be.

130

"But you were leverage from the start. He knew it. I knew it. Even Jack must've suspected."

I feel her shift behind cover. It's just a subtle weight in the air. And I want to rip him apart.

"Don't," I murmur under my breath, more to myself than to her. Because I want to break him. Right here. Right now.

Voss smirks, feeding off the tension.

"Declan died chasing ghosts and hiding secrets. All that loyalty just made him predictable. And predictability?" He shrugs, casual. "That gets people killed."

And I know Voss is wrong.

Dead wrong.

Voss steps closer to her, still circling the moment like it's his to control. "You think you've won? You've made noise, that's all. And noise dies quickly."

Elena doesn't flinch. Instead, she reaches inside her jacket and pulls something out; slowly, deliberately.

A thin, weathered book. Worn at the edges. Marked in a way only those on the inside would recognize.

The original Black Ledger.

She holds it up between them like a torch.

"I'm not a pawn," she says, voice steady. "Not yours. Not Declan's. Not anyone's."

The wind catches her hair, and for a second, Voss's expression slips. Just enough for me to see it.

Fear.

Real fear.

Elena doesn't back down. She steps closer, holding the Black Ledger steady. The one last piece of the truth Declan died to preserve. Inside: facial recognition logs, rerouted accounts, field authorizations. Kill orders with Voss's name stamped clean across the page.

We don't wait.

The trigger's already been set. Sam had built the protocol we launched before we got here.

A soft tone pings in my earpiece. Confirmation of a transmission sent.

Voss doesn't know it yet, but his face, his accounts, and every kill order he authorized are already in the wind.

I step forward just enough for my shadow to stretch across the tarmac.

"It's done," I say, flat and quiet. "The file went live thirty seconds ago. Redacted names, offshore accounts, directive orders with your signature on them. Facial ID. Biometric tags. Contracts tied to Thorne. All of it."

Voss doesn't flinch, but I see it. There is a flicker in his eyes. He knows I'm not bluffing.

"You're going to hear sirens any minute now. Not your men. Not a cleanup crew. Real agencies. Ones you never paid off."

Elena steps in from the side, steady and composed, her presence like a closing gate behind him.

"Every safehouse, every burner credential you've ever used is compromised," I continue. "Every mission you buried under diplomatic seals has been unearthed. And the only reason you're still breathing is because we want you in handcuffs, not as a martyr."

"You think this ends with me?" Voss growls, voice strained.

"No," Elena says. "But it starts with you."

And just then, the wind shifts. It is carrying the faint whine of tires and sirens cutting through the thick Texas air.

Voss doesn't move. But the man at his shoulder, the one who stepped out of the SUV with him, shifts his weight, hand dipping slightly toward the back of his jacket.

"Don't," I say flatly aiming my gun at him before he has the change to pull his own.

Voss man freezes.

Elena appears on his left, weapon up, stance clean. "I would *hate* to mistake a gesture for a threat."

The guard's eyes flick between us, calculations firing behind a calm exterior. But something's off; he's too slow, too resigned.

Voss turns toward him, face hard. "Do it."

But the guard doesn't. Instead, he slowly raises his hands.

"You paid me to keep you safe," he says to Voss. "Not to clean up your mistakes."

Voss snarls and reaches for the inside of his coat.

I move before he can get there.

He's quick, but I'm faster.

I catch his arm mid-reach and drive him hard into the side of the SUV. The vehicle gives a hollow bang, echoing across the tarmac. He grunts, it's loud and sharp, as pain lights up his side.

That wound from the last warning shot we fired, hasn't healed. Good.

He twists, trying to shove me off, but I let the weight of him roll into the motion. I drop low, hook his knee, and bring him face-first to the gravel. My forearm pins the back of his neck.

He spits, teeth gritted. "You think this proves something?"

"Yeah," I mutter. "That you're not untouchable."

Elena's still to the side, weapon steady, trained on the muscle. He hasn't moved, arms half-raised, expression unreadable. If he was ever planning to interfere, he's changed his mind.

A crack of resistance under Voss's ribs makes him howl.

"Jack," Elena warns, voice tight but measured.

I ease up. Just enough to keep control without breaking something else.

Voss coughs, tries to twist again, but his breath catches; ragged and shallow. The ribs are definitely bruised now. Maybe worse.

He's bleeding. And running out of ground.

Then, like he's running on adrenaline alone, he surges up, breaks just enough distance to stagger off the tarmac toward the edge of the brush.

Sirens are closer now. Closing in.

He knows it's over. But he's still trying to outrun the consequences.

Voss coughs once, then spits on the gravel. "You don't get to decide how this ends."

"No," I say with a smile. "But I get to watch it."

He's not getting far. But watching him run feels like the right ending.

Black SUV's roll in. They are government-plated but have no agency markings. Faces we recognize but don't trust. It doesn't matter. The signal flare's already up. We don't know whose badge is in the SUV, but we know enough to stay and watch until he's gone.

Voss is still upright when they reach him. Just barely. He doesn't resist as they cuff him, but he turns to me, eyes burning.

"This doesn't end here," he says.

I believe him.

He's not the kind of man who disappears quietly. The system that made him won't either.

But today, just this once, we're ahead.

Elena slips her hand into mine, fingers cold, grip solid.

And for the first time since this all began, I let myself believe that maybe this isn't just survival anymore.

We're writing the story now.

That's enough.

Chapter 25

A Reckoning

ELENA

It's been three days since they took Voss into custody. Three days of silence and scattered headlines and trying to understand what peace is supposed to feel like when the threat is gone, but the ache still lingers.

Jack stayed behind in Texas to coordinate the final handoff of the Ledger and answer questions to authorities. There had also been fallout to manage. He didn't ask me to stay with him, and I didn't ask him to come back with me.

I needed to do this part alone.

Before returning to the ranch house, I knew we would need supplies, I couldn't even remember the last time we were here for sure. I knew that Tom, Lisa, or one of the other neighbors would have stepped in to care for the animals in our absence, but I felt the need to show up prepared anyway.

I stop in town at the feed store where Tom helps me load up feed and some groceries. Lisa stops by while I am there.

I smell the cinnamon rolls before I see her. "Heard you were coming home. No telling what's left in your fridge, which in case you are wondering is about nothing. Tom and I checked when we were there checking on the animals a few nights ago."

She hugs me and pulls me close. I realize that it in fact might be Lisa that smells like cinnamon. Hugging her though, feels like a home coming. I hug her back.

She hands me the cinnamon rolls, and I smile. "Jack's going to miss out. By the time he gets home, these will likely be gone."

Lisa and Tom both laugh, "I am sure we can manage to bring more," Lisa says.

"Thanks for pitching in unexpectedly."

Tom puts his hand on my shoulder. Strong and heavy, but somehow gentle, "We got you, Elena. And Jack." I drive back to the ranch house with the sun low behind me and a gunny sack full of fresh feed easily accessible in the backseat, just in case Nugget decides to make her opinion known.

The air is different out here. It is not just cooler, but also quieter. The kind of quiet that doesn't press in but stretches wide. Like the land is finally exhaling after everything it held.

I park the jeep in its normal spot near the trees and let myself walk slowly up the drive.

The ranch house is just where we left it. Tucked against the trees, sun-faded in places from the Colorado sun, but solid. Quietly waiting.

I step inside without knocking. Whatever trace of Declan once lingered, real or imagined, is gone. Now it smells like wood smoke and faint herbs, probably one of Jack's teas left behind in the rush. The fire's been cold for days. He hasn't made it home yet. Light filters through the dusty panes like a memory that still cuts too close.

I head straight for the drawer in the bedroom that I never opened.

The drawer's locked, because of course it is. But the key isn't taped underneath like a man with nothing to hide. It's inside a hollowed-out bolt in the back leg of the desk. Typical Declan. Hidden in plain sight, but only if you know how he thinks. I unscrew the head, retrieve the small key tucked inside before sliding it into the lock. It clicks open with a stiffness that says it hasn't been touched in a long time.

Inside the drawer there is one envelope, and my name is on the front. No date. No return address. Just his handwriting; careful, controlled, and a little messier than I remember. I sit down before I open it. Not because I expect it to break me, but because I want to hear him without distraction.

The note is short. Raw. Unfinished in that way all last things are.

Elena,

I know you think I left you in the dark. You're not wrong. I told myself it was to protect you, but maybe it was because I didn't know how to carry it all. I didn't know how to hold you and hold the truth at the same time.

Jack does. I think that's why I trusted him with you, even when I couldn't say it out loud.

He sees you. Not just what you survived, but who you are now. Don't let the world convince you that you need fixing.

You never did.

D.

I don't cry. I just sit with it. Then I fold the page once, careful, and take it outside.

There's a clearing by the edge of the woods, the same spot where the trail meets the tree line. I light the corner with a match from a tin kept by the stove, the kind Jack always carries, and watch the page curl inward, blackening at the edges before disintegrating into ash.

It's not about erasing him. It's about releasing what's left. Guilt. Secrets. Grief.

I return to the ranch house slower, not because I'm heavy, but because I'm lighter. The air feels clearer now too. Each step back from the clearing moves me forward in a different way.

The house comes into view the way it always does; rooted deep like it belongs to the land itself. But this time, I don't just see a house. I see what they built. What Jack kept working to keep alive, even after Declan was gone.

The fencing repaired after every storm. The barn roof patched last fall. The pasture cleared, replanted, and in need of a harvest soon. The cattle Jack had bought at auction this fall, before the steer broke loose.

And the coop, unfinished when I first arrived, now filled with chickens Jack never argued against.

He let me have this. The quiet. The chance to stay. The chickens.

A few of them peck near the porch, feisty little survivors. Nugget among them, still bossing the others around like she owns the place. She probably does.

I kneel, open the gunny sack I had brought home with me, and scatter a scoop of feed from the old tin.

"You stayed," I murmur. "So am I."

The words aren't for them. Just something to fill the stillness, to let them know I will be here.

I pause, watching the way the sunlight hits the dust in the air, soft and gold. It's not peace yet. But maybe waiting means something. Maybe it always did.

I don't hear a warning. Just the quiet rhythm of boots behind me, familiar and certain.

Jack. He's home.

He stops a few paces back. It's not hesitant, just searching. Like he's wondering if there's space for both of us now, not just in the house, but in whatever comes next.

But I know better.

I stand slowly and turn to face him and all that he is. I really take him in, like I never have before. His tall thick rancher build, obviously once a well-defined soldier. His dark hair and thick beard, unlike the pictures of him in his uniforms. Those brown eyes make it hard to breathe, but I step closer to him.

"I didn't come back to be rescued. I came back to choose this. To choose you, Jack."

He exhales. A sound that carries the weight of everything we've lost, and everything we've managed to hold onto.

Then he steps forward, brushing a strand of my hair behind my ear. His thumb slides gently and slowly down my jawline, and I close my eyes. When his hand leaves my face, I open them to see the man standing before me.

There's a stillness in this moment; one I didn't know I was waiting for. Not the silence of grief or distance, but something quieter. Something true. Jack doesn't rush. He doesn't ask. He just sees me. And for the first time, I feel it fully, the closure I didn't know I needed with Declan, and the beginning of something softer with Jack.

Gentle. Steady. And entirely him. He's been weathered by war, shadowed by secrets, but suddenly all I can see is what's been hidden underneath. The quiet strength, the kind heart. Honest. Hardworking. A protector who never asked for thanks. And somewhere beneath all that armor, something softer. Something sweet.

A man who still believes in doing right, even when no one's watching. And he's looking at me like I'm everything.

Not just the man who stood beside me in the fire, but the one I could stand beside now.

Peaceful.

And mine.

The seed of feelings I have felt growing inside, growing into something bigger. Feelings I thought gone after Declan died, growing through the ashes of loss. Something I believe will be beautiful.

"I'm not going anywhere," he says quietly. "Unless it's with you."

Not to rescue. Not to lead. Just to walk beside me.

We don't talk much. We just move together. Down the path, past the barn, toward the open stretch of land that still feels wild and wide and full of things worth choosing. The fields are soft with evening light. The fences strong. The air tastes like dust and grass and everything that says *home*.

This land holds the echoes of what Jack and Declan once dreamed, and the roots of what we're building now.

Not a perfect ending. But a real one.

One we'll build slowly. Together.

JACK

When I come around the bend and see her kneeling on the ground, one hand scattering feed, the other on the gunny sack, I don't just feel relief.

I feel something deeper.

Like all the noise I've carried finally goes still.

She doesn't see me right away. The chickens do. Nugget flutters her wings like she's sizing me up again, ready to remind me who actually owns this place. But Elena… she's just there. Settled. Solid. Like the land finally made space for her and she claimed it without asking.

And God, she belongs here.

Not in the way she once thought. It's not out of necessity, or grief, or because someone offered her a place to land. No. She belongs because she *chose* to.

I stop a few paces back, letting the moment stretch. She stands slowly and turns, her blue eyes soft but sure. The wind catches her hair, and the sun hits just enough to light the edge of her face, like the earth knows she's come home.

I remember every hard thing we survived to get here. Every wall she tore down; not for me, but for herself. Every quiet moment where I could've reached for her but didn't. Not yet.

"I didn't come back to be rescued. I came back to choose this. To choose you," she says.

But now? Now I don't want to wait.

Because what I see in her isn't a woman rebuilding. It's a woman *becoming*. I step forward and brush a strand of hair behind her ear, then gently, almost not touching at all, slide my thumb down her jawline, examining every freckle, every scar, every piece of her I can. She closes her eyes and leans into the moment.

As if she feels the same emptiness I do when our skin stops touching, she opens her eyes.

Elena. Strong. Courageous. Beautiful. Mine, if she'll have me.

And if she lets me, I want to be the man who walks beside her through whatever comes next.

Not to lead. Not to protect. Just to stay.

She's not a weapon anymore.

She's mine.

Not because, I asked. Because she chose.

And for the first time, Elena Dawson is free.

THE END.

If you enjoyed *Disarming Elena,* then you will love *Courting Elena.* Read a sneak peek on the very next page.

Sneak Peek

True North Ranch Book 3

Courting Elena

JACK

They say silence is peaceful. Whoever said that never sat alone on a porch at dawn, listening to the wind move through empty trees and knowing every gust carries the memory of someone you buried too soon.

The morning is cool, early fall cool, he kind that makes your breath visible and the boards beneath your boots creak like they're still deciding if they'll hold your weight. The barn is quiet. The pastures still shadowed. But the sign, *True North Ranch*, catches the light like it's waiting for something. Like it knows.

Declan would've said it's a good omen. That the light lingering on the name meant the day was worth rising for. He used to say a lot of things. Most of them meant something different by the time he was gone.

I sip my coffee and watch the sun climb down the edge of Pikes Peak, lighting the mountains and trees from top to bottom as it crests over the eastern horizon. Our trees. The ones he and I planted before deployment were more symbolic than strategic, back then. Now, they're rooted deep. Just like this place. Just like the woman still asleep inside.

Elena.

Three months ago, I didn't think we'd ever speak again, let alone find a rhythm. Let alone trust. She's not here because of Declan anymore. She's here because she chooses to be.

We've rebuilt fences, repaired the water line, started rotating cattle through the west pasture. She's learning the rhythm of things: the way you check for hoof rot, how to balance feed ratios, what it means when the creek runs faster than usual.

She still calls the chickens her *therapy birds*. Nugget's still a menace. And every morning, there's fresh eggs on the counter before I make it out of the shower.

That's what it has become: ordinary. That in itself is sacred. A rhythm we never say aloud, but one we both move to just the same.

I still hear Declan sometimes; his voice in the back of my mind, in the blueprints left in the shop, in the lockbox I haven't opened since Elena found the envelope. He had his secrets. He thought he was protecting her.

But secrets have a way of growing roots.

The kind that crack foundations if you're not careful.

We've been quiet for a while. I think we both needed that: time to heal, time to work, time to find solid footing again. But last night, Lisa stopped by with a folder she thought I should see. She said it came from one of Declan's old contacts. An old satellite map, a list of names, a note in his handwriting:

"If anything happens, Rourke will come looking for this. Don't let it die in a drawer. Not again."

Rourke. One of Declan's old commanders and my former mentor. A name I haven't heard in almost a decade, until he walked into a meeting last month he shouldn't have been in.

There are lines being drawn that we haven't even seen yet. Elena thinks the past is behind us, but I know better.

And I don't know how long I can keep it from touching her again.

Inside, I hear the floorboards shift. Her footsteps are soft. Deliberate. When she steps out, wrapped in one of my old flannel shirts, mug in hand, she doesn't say anything at first.

I am fairly sure when she folds laundry she picks out my favorite shirts and puts them in her closet. I don't mind, I enjoy seeing her in them.

Elena just looks out at the land.

"I think we need to replant the south corner," she says eventually, nodding toward the field where the wildflowers haven't come back. "Soil's too acidic."

I nod. "I've got lime in the shed."

She sips her tea. Her eyes flick toward me. "You slept at all?"

"Some."

She knows that's a lie. But she lets it pass.

The silence isn't heavy between us. Just full. Like the land itself is holding its breath.

When she leans into my side, I shift just enough for her to fit there naturally. Like she has for the last few weeks, and like I hope she always will.

"There's more coming," I say, my voice low.

She doesn't flinch. Just waits.

"Not sure when. But Declan didn't leave us a map for nothing. Someone's going to come looking."

She exhales slowly. "Then we prepare."

I nod. "We don't run. Not again."

Her hand finds mine.

"No," she says. "This time, we stand our ground."

And for the first time in weeks, I believe we can.

Together.

To get the next book, *Courting Elena,* find it at your favorite book retailer, or scan the QR code below.

And if you feel so inclined, please leave a review of the book on your favorite book platform.

Thank you!

Follow along on social media or visit TessaLeighBooks.com to discover the next book in the series and explore all available titles by Tessa Leigh.

True North Ranch Series:

Defending Elena-When the Match is Lit*

Disarming Elena-When the Flame Takes Shape*

Courting Elena-When the Fire Roars -2026

Women's Domestic Fiction

The Plans They Made Together*

Second Chance Romance Series:

Plans Changed – 2026

*Available in Audiobook

ABOUT THE AUTHOR

Tessa Leigh grew up immersed in the rhythms of military life, moving from place to place, gathering stories and experiences like souvenirs. Surrounded by a family of storytellers shaping her world view, she developed an early love for narratives that explores resilience, transformation, and the unseen connections between people.

A lifelong traveler, Tessa Leigh believes that stories should move the heart and challenge the mind, transporting readers to places both familiar and unknown. Her work blends layered storytelling with thematic depth, crafting worlds where escape and reinvention intertwine.

When not writing, she can be found with her family dreaming up their next adventure to inspire her next artistic endeavor.